The Mailbox : Letters to Grandpapa

Terrie Sizemore

The Mailbox : Letters to Grandpapa
This is a work of fiction.
Copyrighted by Terrie Sizemore ©2025
Library of Congress Control Number: 2022920466

Printed in the United States of America
A 2 Z Press LLC
3670 Woodbridge Rd
Deland, FL 32720
bestlittleonlinebookstore.com
sizemore3630@aol.com
440-241-3126
ISBN: 978-1-954191-84-6

DEDICATION:

To my Grandpapa
I am eternally grateful

Contents

Foreword

The Mailbox : Letters to Grandpa is a novel written by Terrie Sizemore. It's a feel-good read for all ages, including young adult. The main character, Emma, a librarian, writes letters to her deceased Grandpapa and places them in a mailbox set beside his gravesite.

The letters are something she wishes she could share with her beloved grandfather but he's not with her. As she makes her way to see him one day, response letters appear in the mailbox! They are meaningful to Emma so, at first, she doesn't want to know who is sending her letters back.

After a short time, Emma becomes intrigued to know who the letter bandit and writer is.

Emma also wants to adopt twin girls from an orphanage she visits frequently and she falls in love as she navigates life and the adoption process.

1

The Orphanage

"If you're happy and you know it, clap your hands," CLAP CLAP! "If you're happy and you know it, clap your hands," CLAP CLAP! Singing and clapping along, the children finished, "If you're happy and you know it, then your face will surely show it. If you're happy and you know it, clap your hands," ending with a loud CLAP CLAP! Smiles everywhere. We always finish our time with something happy.

I'm Emma Arnold. I frequently visit the 'Gift of Love' Orphanage here in my small neighborhood. I have fallen in love with all these little faces and wish I could take them all home with me. We share story time, snack time, craft time, and play games such as 'duck-duck-goose.' We often have song time, and sometimes we go on outings. The truth is, I could stay with the children every day, all day. Each has a story that breaks my heart.

I cherish the moments I spend with these adorable children. They are happy despite being here without the security of a mom or dad. This is something I understand because, even though I was not a true orphan, I felt like one because I was raised by my grandfather after my parents died in a car accident. Grandpapa is the most wonderful and smartest man I have ever known.

My heart will forever hold dear all my time with him. I'm thankful to infinity and beyond for his devotion and care when I needed it the most. It's been years since I could hug my grandfather and tell him how much I appreciate him for all he did for me. Yet it seems like just yesterday I arrived home to find him on the porch steps, extending his hand to give me money for dinner.

Some of the children are placed here at 'Gift of Love' because they lost *their* beloved parents and had no one to continue caring for them. Others are here for their safety, or their parents are temporarily displaced from their homes. The saddest ones to me are the children who are here because no one wants them. The most precious thing I find among these sweet little faces is how they never seem to complain. They are HAPPY and they know it and their faces surely "show" it!

The orphanage is decorated for the fall season. There's a very large pumpkin in the day room where the children gather for activities and stories. Also inside, are dolls crafted from corn-husks on each table with a pumpkin-scented candle next to the dolls. Garland made of fall-colored orange, red, yellow, and brown leaves are draped around the day room fireplace, and a wreath with the same leaves is perfectly centered on the door leading out of the day room.

Hay bales and dried bundles of wheat stalks are lined up on the front porch. A scarecrow stuffed with straw sits nonchalantly on one of the hay bales, and tall corn stalks are securely tied to the lamppost in the driveway. Everything matches the cool, brisk air of fall.

To top it all off, we're having apple cider and pumpkin spice cookies today. The neighbors dropped off some leftover apples, and the cooks made cider for the children and are planning to make apple pie as well. I enjoy mine warm with ice cream.

Every visit is memorable and a hugely fun time. I'm in deep thought, remembering my Grandpapa as I watch the children bounding around the room. "What are you doing after?" Charlie breaks my trance.

I don't know how long Charlie has worked at the orphanage, but he's been here since I began coming. He is kind to and patient with the children, and I often catch him taking them onto his lap for story time, reassuring them he will always be their friend. He is tall and lanky with dark brown hair and soft hazel eyes. He never speaks loudly to the children, or anyone else for that matter. His low voice calms even me when I arrive in a rush, feeling stressed to make sure I have everything I need and get organized for my time with the children.

Charlie helps me set up and put the snacks out. Sometimes he reads the story to the children as I sit listening. Like me, he especially appreciates holiday stories. This is endearing because most men avoid holiday celebrations and such like the plague. I'm so lucky he assists me.

"Oh, Charlie," I finally respond. "I'm lost in thought. Thanks so much for your help with the children today. They had fun, didn't they?"

"They sure did. They always have fun when you come to see them, Emma." I love Charlie's smile.

"I have a million things to do it seems. I have to run to the bank and post office. Then I'm going to pick up a movie I reserved at the library–one of my faves. I also have to check on my brother to make sure he has meals for the day…"

"Sounds like you're swamped."

"That's an understatement. I don't know how I fit it all in. It seems hectic at times, but since I live so close to everything, it's not so overwhelming." I talk too fast and tend to ramble. Charlie just smiles.

"I have some ideas for activities. Thought we might get together and I can share them with you," Charlie says with a hint of more than just business.

"I'm eager to hear them. Sometimes I can't think of a thing to do, but the children never seem to mind what we do. They just crave the attention we give them and the time we spend."

"That's very true, but I know you. You always want to do something fun and different." It's uncanny how well Charlie seems to know me.

"What works for you?" I ask.

"My schedule is freer than yours. You pick the time and place," he says.

As I reply, "Let me give it some thought," my two little, special, blonde, curly-haired, freckled, favorite three-year-old orphans, Susan and Sarah, rush up for a hug and begin chattering. Charlie realizes this is the end of our casual banter and smiles his usual kind smile.

"And how are my little twin girls? Did you like your story today?" I ask them.

They both shout, "YES!" and happily jump around me. I swoop them both up in my arms, and they giggle and giggle and giggle. We twirl around the room as Charlie watches.

I want to adopt them. I'm not sure of the process, but I really want to adopt them. Somehow I think it is unfair that I have no husband to make us a true family, but at least we would have each other and, even though *here* is lovely, *a life with me would be better than them being here,* I think. Others-namely some of my friends and a family counselor I consulted - disagree. They feel I have too much 'going on' in my life to care for two little girls. *But single parents do it every day,* I say to myself. Anyway, isn't love what life is all about? Everyone says this, but never seems to really mean it.

Susan and Sarah may be twins, but they are nothing alike! Susan is creative and imaginative and uses her talents to draw, color, and paint. She shows me a new masterpiece each time I visit. Today, it's a drawing of me on a horse because I showed her a picture of me on my first horse, my beautiful Solomon. He was a thoroughbred I was lucky to own many years ago. Susan says she wants to ride too. I told her we will ride!! And we will. When I make a promise, I keep it. She also takes pleasure in the outdoors and acts like a tomboy much of the time. She reminds me of myself.

Sarah, on the other hand, is quiet and is a true 'girly-girl' with a somewhat crooked smile. She loves perfume-which she sweetly calls 'pre-fume' and I never correct her, and she spends much time doing her hair. Her curls are free-flowing some days, and some days she puts them 'up' with awkwardly placed clips. She asks if she is beautiful, and I say, "Yes, my dear. You are the most beautiful three-year-old, precious little girl I know!" She always smiles as if these reassuring words make her whole heart smile. She sings and dances with music and, when I play violin, guitar, piano, or cello, she sits close listening as if I'm playing Carnegie Hall! We love our moments together.

When the other children hear me, they ask if they are beautiful too. I exclaim, "You are ALL the most beautiful children I have ever seen in the whole world!" They are happy. I love them all.

And, the truth is, I love both the twins for the beautiful little girls they are. They share a bond that helps them in their young lives together. "You girls are so much fun!" I shout as I put them down. "I'm dizzy and I have to rest!"

"Swing us again," they both beg.

Charlie leaps to my rescue. "I can twirl you," he says.

The girls are happy to have Charlie twirl them because he is so much taller than I am. He throws them in the air and catches them over and over. *He really is perfect*, I think. He never seems to tire of the children. What a wonderful quality.

After twirling the girls, I gather my supplies and clean up. We've had another wonderful morning together. The children head for lunch and nap time.

"Emma, do you have a moment?" The administrator appears out of nowhere.

"Yes, yes…" I stammer.

I follow Mrs. Carter to her office, where she motions for me to take a seat.

"I understand you want to adopt Susan and Sarah," she states matter-of-factly.

"I love those girls. I realize I'm single, but I do wish I could adopt them…." I realize I'm stammering, but I'm caught off guard. I never realized Mrs. Carter knows I want to adopt the girls.

"There's a process…"

"I realize. Do they allow single women to adopt the children?" I ask somewhat sheepishly, but I really need to know.

"Yes. Many single people apply to adopt a child. While we ideally want the children to have traditional homes, we realize not every home is traditional. Love is what matters, right?"

Did she know that's what I think and say? I nod. "That's me alright. In love with those two girls. I actually love all the children here. I wish I could take them all home."

Mrs. Carter doesn't seem shocked or surprised. She smiles. "I've seen you with the children," is all she says.

"I appreciate being able to spend time with them. Thank you for allowing me the privilege to do so."

As I stand to leave, Mrs. Carter shuffles papers and, after not finding what she's looking for, she kindly says, "There is an application packet I thought I had here. I will get one for you to look over. We'll chat soon."

I'm excited and look forward to seeing her again. "Thank you, again," I manage to say and leave her office.

I'm not paying attention as I enter the day room, and I accidentally bump into Charlie. "Is everything alright?" he asks.

"She knows I want to adopt Susan and Sarah, and she's going to get me a packet to look over. I'm still very nervous and don't want the girls to know in case it doesn't work out. You know how things go sometimes."

Charlie nods. "I think you and the girls would make a great family." His smile shows he's sincere – as always.

"I have to get home and write a letter to Grandpapa," I say as I finish packing my supplies.

"Oh, yeah. Letters to Grandpapa," Charlie says wryly.

"What's that supposed to mean?"

"Nothing really. I just know about your letters to your grandfather."

"How do you know?" I'm a little surprised. I don't ever remember telling him about my letters. "Anyway," I ignore that he doesn't answer, "I'd better get home."

"See you soon?"

"For sure," I nod.

I started writing letters to Grandpapa soon after I lost him. I was so sad and devasted. I put up a mailbox right in the spot in the cemetery where he and Grandmama are buried. It seems ghoulish to some, but others think it charming. I think it charming. Mostly, I find it comforting to think I can still connect with him somehow. We talk about everything. I tell him everything, I mean. Today I have much to tell him.

2

The Mailbox: How it All Started

My mind drifts quickly between the past and the present. I remember many years ago, I sat in the practice room and watched with envy as her hands floated effortlessly over the piano keys I struggled so hard to find when I read the rolling black dots on the music pages. She read the notes effortlessly and her fingers just seem to know where to place themselves to make the most beautiful and enchanting music I ever heard. I never asked grandpapa for lessons. Lessons seemed expensive, and we didn't have a piano.

Even today, after playing for years, my hands feel clumsy; my left hand more so than my right. It just doesn't want to cooperate with me the way my right hand does. I try to practice one hand separately and then the other, but still struggle to put them together. They tell me different parts of my brain are responsible for this, but I always wonder how pianists such as her don't seem to have difficulty connecting both parts of their brain to make the music. I always sound like a five-year-old trying to locate the keys. And that's why I practice in private! I hide my secret flaws. If I don't mention them, who will know?

And, as I remember years ago, after I *hear* the music, I can remember how it *should* sound. After my friend left the music room, I spent hours and hours learning to play that song–the one she played instantly and fluently. It is agony for me to get it right, but when I finally play the music, I'm so happy. I never share with anyone how long it takes to play each song. It's slightly easier today than it was so many years ago.

Back to my present thoughts. After I finish practicing my music for the day, I head for the cemetery to talk to Paw. I wrote him a letter and delivered it to him at his mailbox a few days before that read,

> *Dear Paw, I miss you as always. Weather's cool today, sunny though. I spent time remembering High School when I sat with Karen in the practice room listening to her play the piano. I'm still struggling to play. It's still my dream to play better. Sometimes I pretend I'm a concert pianist and the audience is astounded by my expertise on the keyboard, but the truth is the music is slow to come. Sometimes I play it perfectly, but most of the time I make a lot of mistakes. I practice where no one else can hear me, but I wish I were better. Maybe I should quit. Some say I'm not really a musician anyway. What do you think? Wish you were here.*
> *Love, Emma*

I think these are things he would like to know. I always tell him everything. I lost Paw several years ago, but still miss him like it was yesterday when we talked about everything. That's why I put the little mailbox next to his headstone so I can send him letters. I wish everyone knew my grandpapa, and I wish everyone had a grandpapa like mine.

At first, I wrote a letter every day. The mailbox filled up quickly, and word went around town about my little mailbox. Others come to see it, and many feel it's a sweet way to remember the ones we lose. In fact, I think it has been an inspiration for many others to put up their own mailbox so the grandchildren can write letters to their grandmamas and grandpapas.

As I walk the long streets to the cemetery today, the piano music swirls around in my head. I imagine my hands on the keyboard and think of all the other musicians I have watched play. They all make it look so simple and easy. I'm happy with my meager progress today.

A friend suggested I play the violin because I would only have to play one note at a time. I think talented violinists play multiple notes at one time, but I don't need to play more than one note to enjoy the instrument. I may even consider the cello and viola too!

On cool days like this late-October day, the wind picks up quickly and blows my hair so. I'm slightly chilled, so I zip up my bulky, oversized sweater to ward off the brisk winds. The walk takes me past a large park I occasionally visit. It's a place where I can sit and think about life and the world revolving around me. The daily news never seems pleasant. I don't watch much of it, but when I do, I'm glad to feel safe in my little area of the world. I'm so lucky, so blessed- as if perhaps I've been given more than my share.

Today, the park is filled with dogs of every breed. When I look closely, I see they're having a dog show. *Why did they pick such a cool day*? I wonder. The dogs don't seem to mind the brisk wind.

I am thrilled to see the dogs all trimmed real fancy and trotting like they're prancing next to their owners who want their pet to win the blue ribbon. No matter what anyone says, there's nothing like the feeling of 'first place.' It's rare for me, but really nice. Once, I won a blue ribbon for a cross-stitch piece I entered in a sewing contest at the county fair. No one remembers but me, but I was proud to receive that ribbon!

My favorite breed in the show today is the Dachshund. They are spunky and sassy, and I appreciate this about them. I think it's amusing to see the 'hounds' all lined up and, after all the larger dogs, at the end of the line is where we see the small Dachshund. They are so cute standing proudly on their short, little legs, waiting to be judged. They have my vote.

The atmosphere in the park is cheerful today. There are many booths sending the aroma of delicious food into the air as I pass. It reminds me of the day Paw and I went to the county fair. We each had sausage sandwiches covered with red sauce, onions, and green peppers. Yum! We enjoyed everything at the fair that day. I especially adored the children's crafts and art and watching them with their 4-H animals. Once I saw a young boy cleaning a rooster's legs and feet. He was using a toothbrush to clean the grooves. Children naturally do the most amazing things with animals. They are fearless and just seem to believe the animal will allow them to do anything. In another area, a young girl was blow-drying her chicken, who was letting her do this with skinny eyes from the warm air blowing on it.

I want to stray from my path a little to have a snack before arriving at the cemetery, but I don't. I tighten my grip on my sweater and continue head-on into the wind gusts to make my way past the park. The wind calms a little.

As I cross over the highway, the sounds of trucks and diesel engines fill the air, as well as the fumes from their exhaust. This is not the most enjoyable part of my walk to the cemetery, but at least it's only a short part of the jaunt.

I finally arrive at the enormous arches that welcome visitors into the 'Riverside Cemetery.' "I'm almost there, Paw," I say under my breath.

When I come to where my beloved Grandfather is laid to rest, I usually sit on the grass near his headstone. Today it's a little wet, so I elect to stand. "Alexander"…. it reads–"from ….. to….." and "Beloved Husband and Father." It should say BEST GRANDFATHER EVER because he is the best and most beloved Grandfather in the entire world. I'm certain everyone would agree if they knew him for only five minutes.

My visits allow me to feel close to him. As I talk and talk to him, I look around and notice a beautiful spread of red roses leaning against a nearby headstone. *WOW!* I think. *Someone brought really beautiful flowers for their loved one.*

Today, I brought a miniature, beautiful white rose for

my Grandpapa. I'm thankful for God blessing me with this to bring. I'm certain my small flower shared with my Paw would be seen as BIG if they only knew him!

As I look at the small mailbox sitting next to my grandfather's headstone, I notice a small white paper inside. *My notes are always on light pink paper. What's this?... I muse.*

I reach into the mailbox, remove the paper, and read the note. I'm speechless, and a small, soft, and warm tear rolls down my cheek. "Thank you, Paw," I whisper.

But how did this note get into Paw's mailbox? This never happened before. This is a small cemetery, and I rarely see others visiting here. I hold the note to my chest and look around, hoping to find someone watching and, at the same time, hoping I won't find someone watching. A rush of unexpected happiness comes over me. It's amazing how words can comfort and encourage one when they need the words the most.

As I pass the park on my way home, the dogs have all gone. The park seems lonely with no one there, but it will be filled again with the hustle and bustle of activity. I'm certain of this. The ebb and flow of people coming and going and enjoying this little park is an absolutely assured truth.

When I arrive home, I'm happy to be out of the wind and cool weather. I prepare hot water for tea with honey–just what I need when I'm chilled. I still have the little note from Grandpapa's mailbox. I decide on a special place for it.

I rummage through my boxes and jars and finally find a small tin box labeled, 'TREASURES.' I'm a saver and have held onto many things from my childhood and every season of my life. I have a lot of stuff!

I'm criticized for being such a saver–or hoarder, some may say-but I hide these things about myself. It's easier that way. These little things are precious to me, so I keep them.

I dust off the small tin box and place the sweet note inside. *Now, I have to find a place for this box,* I tell myself. I find a place between the many knick-knacks I have been given over the years.

The space I find is near my kitchen window. It will remind me of the precious words I can't imagine how they arrived in Grandpapa's mailbox, but I sure am glad they did. I set the box down and fix my green tea.

I sip my tea with tupelo honey because Grandpapa told me this is my father's favorite honey, so now it's my favorite honey. Grandpapa told me so many stories about my mom and dad. I remember each story.

I gather my supplies for art class tomorrow. I'm a children's librarian and, on my break twice a month, I do art!

I set out my brushes, palette, paints, smock, and paper. *What will we create tomorrow?* I'm always excited about a new project. I think the instructor mentioned we're painting birds this lesson. There are endless ideas for art! I know it will be great.

3

Art Lessons

I tell myself I should be more diligent about breakfast and agree with those who feel it's an important meal. I regret that Paw and I had donuts more often than we should have. I do a little better now, but not much. I sleep as long as I can, so breakfast suffers. I scarf down a bowl of cereal or something else easy to fix so I make it to work at the library on time. Sometimes I have home-baked cookies, buttered toast, or just a glass of orange juice. Sipping juice at work gives me the feeling I'm being healthy even when I should be more conscientious. I have it on my list to work on a healthy diet. My list is long.

Each morning, I enjoy watching the birds that visit the birdfeeder outside my kitchen window. I like the cardinals best because they remind me of my father. I didn't know him well or for long, but he was a bird watcher. I think they're called 'birders.' When I was five-years-old, he took me bird watching and taught me about robins, sparrows, blue jays, and beautiful cardinals. Tragically, I lost my parents when I was seven. That's when I went to live with my dear Grandpapa.

I was visiting my aunt the day the accident happened. The police came to the door, and my aunt and uncle began crying. I heard soft words, but I couldn't make out what they were saying. After the police left, my aunt turned to me and said, "Emma, you're going to stay with Auntie for a while." I was confused, but I loved her, so I was happy to stay.

After a few days, I knew something was different. My parents hadn't come home, and no one wanted to talk much. Auntie bought me a new dress and we went for a car ride to a place I had never been before. "Before we go in, Emma, I need to tell you something very sad. There was a terrible accident, and both your parents were hurt badly. The doctors and nurses tried *very* hard to help, but your mom and dad died. They won't be coming home anymore. I know you may not understand this, but we're here for you. You can live with your Grandpapa. How does that sound?"

A small tear fell down my right cheek. I nodded and, as my lips trembled, I said, "Yes. Grandpapa, please."

When we walked into the building, everyone there was sad and gathered in a big open room where my mom and dad were placed in what looked to me like long, brown boxes.

I never saw a person who wasn't alive, so I didn't know how to respond. Part of me understood my parents were never coming back, and I cried. People kept patting my head and saying, 'Poor little thing.' Grandpapa took me in his arms and said, "Angel, you're coming home with me." He twirled me and made me laugh so I wasn't so sad anymore. I hugged his neck as hard as I could.

As I recall those long-ago days, the male cardinal visiting today seems to know I'm watching him. He snatches some seeds quickly and then flies away. Another flies by but doesn't stop for the seed, while several very small birds come for breakfast. If I had time, I would pull my book out to see if they are sparrows or wrens or some other sweet little bird. I'm running just on time, so I have to get going with my morning. I've spent enough time with my memories.

I pack my lunch, which today consists of a ham sandwich with cheese, tomato, lettuce, and mayo on whole wheat bread, an applesauce cup, and a few celery sticks.

On my lunch break, I'm going to slip out to the art class I've been looking forward to all weekend. If I'm correct, we'll be using watercolors to create a painting of birds. This is one reason I especially enjoyed watching them outside my window this morning. Catching glimpses of them will help me paint beautiful birds today.

My favorite medium is watercolor. I've tried using acrylics and pencils, but I always seem to drift back to watercolor. I've never dabbled in oils but think they're something I may want to learn to paint with sometime.

In addition to lunch, I pack the brushes, palette, smock, and the paper I gathered last night. It's off to the library.

Today is a great day at the library. Not only am I going to art class on break, I scheduled an art project with a kindergarten class that comes to the library frequently as part of their lessons.

This is helpful because I dressed for this activity and my art class. I'm wearing my red-rimmed glasses and painter's palette earrings. My designer-styled blue jeans and white t-shirt dress are casual in case I splatter paint on myself during the kindergarten activity or in my art class. I have a bulky sweater to cover up my t-shirt when we're not in an art session. I don't want others to consider me *sloppy*.

I cherish every minute of being a librarian. Books interesting because they're filled with stories that make me laugh and cry, sometimes at the same time. Books also teach me things about myself, others, and the world around me. I enjoy sharing them with others. As a librarian, I get to do this daily.

Books open a path for each reader to educational information, adventure, self-help, and more. I read many different types of books. When I want to laugh, I read something funny. When I want a mystery – enough said.

Sometimes I'm interested in educational books. For instance, I once read a book about trigonometry because I didn't understand it when I studied physics. I heard about a man who wrote a book about walking the Appalachian Trail, so I wanted to read his hilarious story.

Sometimes I prefer fiction, sometimes non-fiction. The beauty of books is that there's a book for everyone! I chose to be a children's librarian because I'm passionate about children's picture books.

Picture books are not only entertaining for the young readers, most of the time they are a child's first introduction to reading. Picture books tell stories to young readers and help them learn to read and understand language. They make reading fun and not drudgery, and are a stepping stone for more advanced reading. Did I mention they're fun?

The library is only two short blocks from my home, so I bundle up on this cooler-than-yesterday morning and head to work. I call it *my* library because it feels like home to be surrounded by all these wonderful books, and I'm the head librarian in the children's section.

The library was renovated recently. They added a large children's area where I spend my day. The atmosphere is casual. There are computers for personal use, quiet areas for children to study, and the library placed a few bean-bag chairs around for the children who want to stay a while and read books without taking them home.

The shelves are stacked with my beloved colorful picture books that are filled with all different stories. Some stories are cute 'just-for-fun' stories, some have meaningful messages and lessons we value, some are about accepting others who may be different from us, and some are educational. My library is busy with children visiting throughout the day to borrow a special book.

"Good morning, Peter," I say to my fellow librarian.

"Morning, Emma," he retorts as he continues sorting the books returned overnight. "You're looking pretty dapper this morning," he adds without looking my way.

"Thanks. We have art with the kindergarteners today, as well as I have art class at lunch," I say as I feel my face flush. I change the subject to, "And when is story time today? Do you know?" I ask.

"I think it's in about twenty minutes. Is art with the children before or after lunch?"

"After lunch, thankfully. I'd better pick a book for

story time. Do you have anything in mind?" I ask.

Peter stops, looks a little exasperated, thinks for a moment, and then picks *The Little White Kitten and Her Little Red Mittens* from the stack of books he's sorting. "Here, this is a good one. A classic," he says as he hands me the book.

The Little White Kitten and Her Little Red Mittens is one of my favorites. It's a good pick for story time. I set it on my desk and organize my lunch and art supplies. I don't notice any phone messages, so that's a relief. I read two emails regarding book availability. I stack some stray pens in a flower-pot pencil and pen holder that the children at the orphanage made for my birthday in May this year. It's a terracotta pot that they painted purple and yellow flowers on. They added a few green leaves and, overall, did a sweet job decorating it for my 'work desk' they told me it is for. I cherish it because I think of them all day when I see the pot filled with pens and pencils.

"Do you want to read to the children today, Peter, or do you want me to?"

"Either way. I can read if you want me to," Peter stated. He's easy to work with and always willing to pitch in. Peter is someone everyone likes. He looks right at you when he speaks to you. He is patient and never rushes through a conversation. Today he's dressed in a pair of navy pants and a white shirt with a blue and black checkered tie. His clothes cover his nicely built physique that is pretty awesome because he works out regularly. He always looks dressed up. His dark hair is perfectly groomed, and I swear I always detect a little twinkle in his dark brown eyes.

"I'll turn story time over to you. I'm dressed for art class today. I hope you don't get paint on your nice clothes this afternoon," I say with a smile and hand the book back to him.

Peter smiles back at me and then continues restocking the books in their correct position so the next young reader can locate them.

Just before story time, Peter changes and dresses as a

pirate and, after reading *The Little White Kitten and Her Little Red Mittens,* he and the children roam the library looking for letters of the alphabet. It's a game he plays with the children looking for A, B, C, and all the way to X, Y, and Z. He cleverly hides clues and has all the letters and alphabet books low enough for the younger children to find easily.

As Peter and the children play alphabet treasure hunt, I meet with the head librarian for our weekly connect. Then, it's time for lunch. I gather my art supplies and head to class. I work close to the art store, so I scarf down my sandwich on my walk over.

"Hello, ladies," I say as I enter the art store.

"Hi, Emma," they say almost in unison. They don't comment on my dress because they're used to seeing me in 'art' clothes, and they're all dressed casually as well.

"Sit anywhere you want, Emma. The class is smaller today, but we still have about eight ladies joining us," Louise says, today's instructor.

As we settle in and place our supplies at our work areas, I don my smock. Even though I dressed casually, I don't want to have paint splatter on my clothes. It makes me feel as if I'm a real painter when I wear my smock. I know it's silly. I remember seeing pictures of artists in their smocks, like Egon Schiele of Gustav Klimt's painting in his painter's smock, and Vincent Van Gogh's self-portrait in a blue smock.

During class, I first draw the birds in pencil. Then I add a couple of trees, a small bird feeder that resembles mine at home, some bushes, and one flowering plant. I intend to put red flowers on this one flowering plant because I know red will brighten the picture.

Then comes the color. I paint a blue sky and green grass. I make sure there's detail and shading in the sky and grassy areas. Next, I start painting my bird. I see how other artists in the class mix paint to the 'just perfect' color needed for the realistic feathers and heads of the birds. I try mixing colors of paint, but my colors seem to be either the original colors I started with or some awful muddy brown color I don't like. I decide to use different shades of blue and light brown to paint my bird's feathers and add some shading, or blending of the colors, as Louise says. Then I fill in the trees and branches and scatter leaves over them. I paint the bush and then add the red to my one flowering plant.

As I look over my painting, I'm pleased. The bird is brilliantly blue and has shades of tan running through its feathers. The trees actually look like trees, and the leaves are different shades of green. When I first started painting, the trees just looked like globs of green paint. I think I've come a long way.

I'm happy with my work until I see the other students' paintings. These women are so talented. Their art looks like a perfectly crafted photograph. The details are stunning, and the artists put every stroke of detail in with meticulous precision. I secretly envy their talent. Don't get me wrong, I don't think I'm envious to a fault, I'm happy they're so talented. I just wish I had their talent. Their birds look more realistic than mine, and the shading and colors are perfectly detailed. It seems I can see every vein on every leaf in their paintings, and the sky is a perfect shade of sky-blue with scattered clouds. Before I can stow my picture into my art folder, Louise walks over.

"Your picture is lovely, Emma," Louise tells me.

"Not quite as lovely as everyone else's," I reply with my nose scrunched. I think she's just being kind, and I want to be honest.

"That's not true, Emma. You're being too hard on yourself. You've come a long way. You did a really nice job. The bird is drawn accurately and you painted it wonderfully. The bush is in proportion and painted as nicely as well as your red flowers." She smiles sincerely as she nods her head, 'yes.' I feel better. Perhaps I am too hard on myself.

I still wish I had just a little more talent. My fondness for art isn't a substitute for talent, but I do so enjoy creating art. I will write Grandpapa about all this.

I arrive back at work and return calls about books that

a few moms called to inquire about. Then, before art with the children, I write my letter to Grandpapa:

> *Dear Paw, I miss you more than usual. I went to art class today at lunch. I painted a small picture of a bird in a tree with a bush and a red flowering plant. When I looked over at the other ladies' pictures, I wished my art looked like theirs. The instructor said my work is special because it's something I created. I think she was just trying to make me feel better. Remember my first art class, where I was frozen and wouldn't even pick up the brush because I thought I couldn't do it? That was some time ago. You know how much I love art. It makes me happy. Maybe I should quit. Some say I'm not really an artist anyway. What do you think? Wish you were here. Love, Emma*

After writing my letter to Grandpapa, I see the ten kindergarteners coming through the door, prepared for art class. Their mothers are quite smart. They dressed their children for a messy activity today. Caleb walks over to me and says, "My mom made me wear my dad's old t-shirt for painting today."

"I see," I say, chuckling. "It's a good idea. We may get some paint on our clothes today."

The children take seats at the activity table, and Peter and I pass out the small canvases we're going to work on today. We decide to make thumbprint caterpillars with the children because it should be the least messy activity we can think of.

We show the children how to dip their first finger into the blue fingerpaint and then press onto the canvas, leaving a small blue print. Then we do the same with the red, yellow, and green paints, making a continuous body of our caterpillars. Peter and I give the children thin black magic markers and show them how to put the dots for eyes and use small strokes for legs on each colored thumbprint and two black strokes on the head for antennas.

"Look at mine," Olivia says, showing me her thumbprint caterpillar.

"This is beautiful!" I exclaim. "I'm passing around little wooden easels for you to put your canvas painting on to take home."

Each child takes an easel and carefully puts their colorful caterpillars on them. They are so pleased. Peter and I are pleased as well. We are most pleased because we enjoyed the painting event without getting any paint on ourselves. This is monumentally great.

The children leave and, before I head home, I comb the shelves in the adult section of the library for a new and exciting book to take home. As a young girl, I reveled in horse books. Walter Farley's *Black Stallion* series was my fave. I dreamt of being a jockey and winning the Kentucky Derby! A dream that went to the wayside when I grew taller and heavier than jockeys are allowed to be. But it was fun to read the books that brought that dream to me. What would life be without our dreams? And the books that help us dream?

I choose an interesting book in the non-fiction section about a doctor's journey to becoming a heart surgeon and decide this is my new before-bedtime read. I sign it out and tuck it into my backpack.

"Any plans tonight, Emma?" Peter asked.

"Not much. Going to visit Grandpapa, and then I want to get ready for my visit to the orphanage tomorrow. How about you?"

"My usual. Home to a TV dinner, the news, and an early evening," Peter says.

"You could always come with me tomorrow to the orphanage. We are having a pumpkin party. You're great with kids. By the way, the children really enjoyed *The Little White Kitten and Her Little Red Mittens* today. And, I saw you do your pirate routine searching for the alphabet letters. Very nice, Peter."

"Thanks. I might just join you. It sounds as if you have a nice time with the children. What sparked your interest in the orphanage?"

I think carefully before I respond. "I was basically an orphan myself. After my parents died in a car accident, I went to live with my grandpapa. He was wonderful. I would have had nowhere to go if he hadn't stepped in to take me home with him." I stopped a moment. I never told Peter this before. "Our home is close to the orphanage. I would see the children playing when I passed by. A few years ago, I stopped in and asked if I could spend time with the children. When I told them I was a librarian and wanted to read to the children, they were excited and invited me to lead story time. Then I added a craft and a snack afterward. I started adding other projects and occasionally an outing. We sing too."

"You're doing a good thing." Peter seems impressed.

"I enjoy my time with the children. I think about those little ones every day and plan something special when I can. In fact, I'm planning a pumpkin carving contest–well, not really a contest-but a party. They look forward to these activities."

"I'm sure the kids will enjoy that. And, I'm sure you will too." I love it when Peter smiles.

"I would really appreciate your help," I say.

"For sure," Peter says. "I'd be happy to join you for the pumpkin party."

"That's great! I'd appreciate your help very much. You do know I'll put you to work, don't you?"

Peter laughs and says, "I think I can live with that."

"And we will have snacks for all your help. Oh, look at the time. I better be off to the cemetery. See you tomorrow?"

"For sure," Peter says.

I pack my things and head for the cemetery. The park is buzzing again with children swinging and running around after each other. Sometimes I think their shrieks can be heard for miles. I smile and watch them as I continue my walk.

When I arrive at Grandpapa's site, I slip my note into the mailbox. "Good evening, Grandpapa," I start. "I have a very important note for you today. I hope you are well where you are. I know you're always looking down on me. You know I miss you as much as always and always will."

I sit and chat for a few more minutes and, suddenly, out of the corner of my eye, I think I see someone dart behind one of the statues in the distance. *I wonder who that is?* I'm slightly frightened because I'm usually the only one in the cemetery - or so I thought. For a few minutes, I stare in the direction I think I saw someone, but don't see any other movement. *Must have been a bird or the wind or something,* I tell myself and dismiss it altogether.

"Well, Paw, I'm heading home. I'm going to see Susan and Sarah tomorrow, those cute twins I told you about. The other children are cute too, and I wish I could take all of them home with me. I tell you this every time I see you, but I know you don't mind."

I get home pretty quickly and slip into warm, comfy bedclothes. Home. The home I shared with my grandpapa. It is the same as the day he brought me here, except a new appliance here or there. A new television, too. There is a true comfort in feeling like he's still here, and I have this attachment to him that no one can take away.

Dinner is a healthier meal than breakfast because I have more time to devote to making it. Tonight, it's salmon with asparagus and small, organic boiled red potatoes with butter and parsley.

Then, I gather my thoughts for the pumpkin carving party with the children at the orphanage tomorrow. It warms my heart when I see them all excited. I have to admit I'm excited too!

I'm hoping seventeen children will join the fun. Each year, I buy just the right-sized pumpkins for their little hands. I also have small-scale carving kits that are safe for the children that I keep from year to year. I like cute things, and these little carving kits are cute. They have a little spoon to scoop out the 'inners' of the pumpkin and a child-safe carving tool to make the faces.

The children can make funny faces and, did I mention, we'll all have a fun time! I have been having a pumpkin party for years for various groups of children. Charlie let me know the orphanage has cider and pumpkin cookies for treats for the workers and the children.

As I always say, I'm excited about this and, before I can finish my lists, check all my supplies, and get packed, I fall asleep.

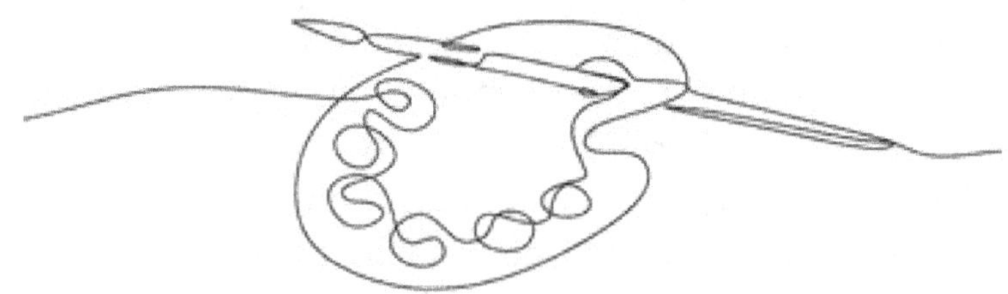

4

Adoption Papers
and Pumpkins

I only work until 2:00pm on Wednesdays, which gives me plenty of time to organize projects for the little ones at the orphanage. Today is pumpkin carving day. My old red metal wagon is loaded down with the twenty small pumpkins I picked up at the farmers' market on Saturday.

This little red wagon is special to me because it's the wagon Grandpapa gave me. It's the one I toted all my dolls and stuffed animals in for many years. When Paw gave me my first German Shepherd puppy, Eddie, I pulled him around in it as well. Now, many years later, it has a few small dents and a little rust, but these are barely noticeable.

I also fill two canvas bags with my decorating and carving supplies. One bag holds the carving kits for the older kids, and the other has washable markers and stickers for the younger ones. I'm off to the library! Did I mention we're going to have fun!

Today I wear my orange-rimmed glasses. I have many pairs of glasses. These are round-shaped and are quite stylish. I also wear pumpkin earrings I think will be festive today. If I had a pumpkin costume, I think I would wear it, but I don't. So, I have to settle for a sweater with fall-colored leaves on it and my orangish-colored jeans.

My friend and fellow librarian, Peter, did offer to come

along. I will hold him to it because we're going to need all the helping hands we can get. Over a dozen children, six bottles of paint, seventeen pumpkin carving kits, and twenty pumpkins that need to be scooped out and carved. What could go wrong?

Work goes by quickly. It's time to head over to the orphanage.

Still planning on coming today, Peter?"

"Sure. Do you want me to bring anything?"

"No. I have everything, but would you mind helping me take it all over?" I ask in a *please don't say no* tone with a begging look.

"How could I refuse?" Peter smiles wryly.

"You can't. So, do you want to pull the wagon or carry the bags with the kits and stickers?" I ask.

"Which is more helpful? I think pulling the wagon with all those pumpkins would be more helpful." Peter takes the handle and slowly moves the wagon filled with pumpkins. "It's heavier than it looks," he laughs.

"I know. Who would think twenty small pumpkins would weigh that much? I bought a few extra in case we have more children. You're welcome to carve one if you want."

"We'll see," he responds as he continues pulling the wagon.

We trudge to the orphanage and are greeted by all the children talking at once. "Who's this?" young Andrew asked, pointing at Peter.

"This is Peter. He's going to help today. We have a BIG project! We're going to carve and decorate pumpkins that you can put in your windows. Doesn't that sound fun?" I have everyone's attention.

"Yeah!" they all agree with happy faces.

Charlie arrives with his usual sweet smile. "How can I help?" he asks.

"I'm so glad to see you. Can you bring the kids to the activity room in about ten minutes? I'll have everything set up, and then we can have them pick out their pumpkins and get started with a carving or decorating kit," I say in my stressed voice.

"Will do." Charlie readily agrees and begins helping the children find their places. He turns to me and adds, "It's all going to be okay," knowing I need the reassurance. I smile.

Peter rolls the wagon filled with pumpkins into the activity room while I cover the long tables with newspaper and set out the supplies. The kids stream in and immediately run for the pumpkins. Charlie follows with an apologetic look. "Sorry, Emma. I couldn't hold them back any longer. They're a little excited."

Sure, I think. Charlie looks just as excited as the kids. I smile and say, "I am too. It's okay."

This is not going as I planned. I had visions of calling the children one by one to come up and calmly choose a pumpkin. I forget that little ones are not the most patient people. I smile more as I see everyone's enthusiasm, and I quickly abandon my plans.

Peter steps out of the way as the kids swarm the wagon. He doesn't want to become an early casualty.

"I missed you, Miss Emma," Sarah says as she gives me a hug.

"Me too," Susan chimes in.

"My two sweet little girls!" I exclaim and hug them back. "How are you today?"

"Good! Can you pick us to win best pumpkin?" Sarah asks.

"Yeah. Please pick us," Susan adds.

"Well, I think we're just having fun today and not picking best or not-best pumpkins. How's that?"

"OK!" they both say together loudly and race over to pick out their pumpkins.

It's fun to see each child choose their pumpkin. The children range in age from three to twelve. Some of the youngest ones want the biggest pumpkins! "Tony! I think that pumpkin is too big for you, sweetheart," I say as I rescue him from being crushed beneath the largest pumpkin I brought.

"I can do it, Miss Emma," Tony assures me.

"Alright. I'm going to ask one of the assistants to be close, Tony," I say as Julie, one of the long-time workers at the orphanage, raises her hand to volunteer to watch over and help Tony with his pumpkin.

Angie looks for the 'ugliest, bumpiest one,' while a few others choose based on color. Even though the rush seems like chaos to me, each child is happy with their choice, and the process certainly goes much quicker than if I chose one child at a time to pick a pumpkin.

"OK. Everyone, please sit down." With palms down, I use this universal sign for the children to quiet down and sit. The last of the pickers eventually straggle back to their seats, clutching their pumpkins. They are so cute. They squirm in their seats as they look at me, Charlie, and Peter expectantly.

"Charlie and Peter are going to give some of you a little kit to use to carve your pumpkins," I say.

Charlie passes the carving kits to the older children that include tiny little safe saws. Some are straight while others have curved blades. "These are cool," he comments.

"Yes. I think they're pretty cool too. They make it easy for the children to have safe fun. With supervision, of course." Charlie already understands we all need to keep our eyes on the kids.

Peter hands out the decorating kits with stickers for the younger children's pumpkins.

After all the supplies are distributed, Charlie and Peter help cut the tops off the pumpkins. I give each child a big metal spoon to scoop out the guts. They roll up their sleeves and are excited to get started. Well, most of them.

Andrew can't bear to touch the slimy pumpkin seeds. Ben wants to see how far he can spit the seeds. Susan is racing to empty her pumpkin the fastest, and Sarah talks Charlie into scooping out her pumpkin for her.

Evan gives up on the spoon entirely and decides it's easier to stick his arm all the way into the pumpkin and scoop with his fingers. He pulls out a fistful of pumpkin seeds and stringy guts and holds it all up in the air as if he were showing us an Olympic trophy. His arm and hand are covered in slimy pumpkin 'inners.'

"Ooh, you're dripping it on me," Bennie complains as he pushes Evan's arm away. Evan windmills his arms to keep his balance, causing pumpkin guts to fly across the table ... and splooshes Peter right in the face with a stringy yellow wad.

Without saying a word, Peter slowly picks seeds off his eyebrows and goo out of his shirt collar. Uh oh. I can only imagine how Peter's feeling because he is always so 'prim and proper.'

I can't help myself. "Peter, Peter, Pumpkin Eater." Oops, maybe I've gone too far. Peter doesn't look happy as he slowly releases air from his nose. I suspect he is counting to ten.

Suddenly, Charlie grabs a massive chunk of pumpkin goo off the table and plops it right on his head, yelling, "Look at me, I've been slimed!" The room erupts with the loud, glorious laughter of over a dozen children and one amused librarian.

It's happy bedlam after which most of the kids want to get in on the act. I'm touched that good-ol'-Charlie has lightened the mood by making himself the messy joke.

"Alright. Everybody stop and listen," I say after a few more moments of play and trying to take control again. I need their attention. "I think we should wash up a little and then finish the pumpkins." Everyone agrees.

The children are accustomed to lining up and heading to the wash-up areas, so they're orderly and well-behaved. After washing their slimy little hands, they return to their pumpkins.

I help Peter clean up too. He doesn't seem too worse for wear. A few wet paper towels do the trick. "I'm so sorry, Peter," I start to say.

"It's OK, Em. I wasn't expecting this, but I can deal with it." He smiles a sincere smile and I know he's alright.

"Next, we're going to make the faces. You can make any face you want on your pumpkin. You can make a scary face," I say as I bare my teeth and growl. "You can make a silly face," and I cross my eyes and tilt my head. "Peter and Charlie and I will help with whatever face you choose."

As we finish carving and decorating the pumpkins, I walk around the table and pick up each pumpkin to show the others. When I pick up Lisa's pumpkin, I'm so surprised and make much over it. "Look how cute this is." Lisa made faces all around the pumpkin, not just one face! I never saw someone carve a pumpkin like this before. "This is really cute!"

Before I can stop myself, I think I hurt the other children's feelings as I make so much over Lisa's pumpkin. The truth is, they are all darling. I am just happily surprised with Lisa's and obviously say so. I promise myself to never do this again. I want every child to feel special, so I immediately go around to each child and say something nice about their pumpkins.

When I pick up Evan's pumpkin, I see he didn't carve a face; he just made two large, uneven holes for the eyes. "Oh, Evan, what a good idea. You've made your pumpkin look totally surprised!" Evan smiles proudly.

Bernie doesn't want his pumpkin hollowed out. Instead, he used the stem as a big, curly nose. He drew eyes above and a tiny mouth below. "Bernie, your pumpkin is looking up at heaven. Such a great idea." Bernie looks at his shoes and smiles despite himself.

"You have all done such lovely pumpkins. Do you like them?"

"WE DO!" All the children chime in together.

"Are we going to have a story and a snack today, Miss Emma?" Adam asks.

"Yes, Adam. We are going to have a snack now. Peter has volunteered to read our story." I try to stay positive after his earlier bout with pumpkin guts.

"Yeah!" Adam raises both arms in glee.

"We have peanut butter and jelly sandwiches today with sliced apples and milk." I'm not sure where the cider and cookies went, but the children don't mind healthy snacks, and the orphanage tries to source the freshest ingredients as well.

After snacks, I call and wave to the children, "Let's all come to the story rug."

They're slightly tired, but they all move from the snack tables to the rug. Peter has *Joey Visits the Pumpkin Patch* in his hand.

"These children will enjoy this," I say, encouraging Peter.

"I hope so," Peter replies.

Susan and Sarah curl up on my lap. Thankfully, they are small and fit just right. We all listen to Peter as he reads *Joey Visits the Pumpkin Patch*.

After story, I remind the children, "Tell Peter *thank you* for reading today."

The children thank Peter and hug him. I think these are the hugging-est children there have ever been. They love to hug, and we never refuse.

"Time for a nap," one of the other assistants calls. The children line up and off they go.

"See you next time, girls," I say to Sarah and Susan as they jump from my lap, give a hug, and head to nap time.

After the children leave, Charlie says, "Pretty cool pumpkin carving today, Emma."

"Glad you liked it. It's a great fall activity for the children," I say. "Did you meet Peter?"

"Sort of. Hi, I'm Charlie," Charlie says as he shakes hands with Peter.

"Peter."

"Sorry about all the mess. The children can be quite spunky sometimes," Charlie says, trying to diffuse the situation.

"It's OK. I'm not upset. It has been a fun day, really. I'm glad I came."

Peter's being a good sport, I think.

"How long have you known Emma?" Charlie asks.

"We work together at the library," Peter says.

"Great," Charlie responds.

I sense a little suspicion in his voice, but I disregard it and say, "Well, I want to thank you both for your help. I couldn't have done this without you. I sure do enjoy these children, and you made this possible. Thank you again and again. I'm so sorry about the mess…"

Both Charlie and Peter smile. I know they're happy to help. I've been friends with both of them for some time. I see Charlie at the orphanage and Peter at work. Both are nice to me. I leave it at that.

"So, Emma, can you spare some time to discuss some activities and Thanksgiving?" Charlie asks.

"Sure. What works for you?"

"How about we meet here tomorrow evening for a chat. Can I bring dessert?"

"Sounds great. Is there anything you'd have me bring?" I ask.

"No. Just yourself." He smiles.

I gather my now-empty wagon and my bags of dirty and opened supplies. It's time to make my way home to clean myself and my things up before my visit to Grandpapa.

A little while later, I arrive at Grandpapa's and check the mailbox. No new letters. I take my new letter from my jacket pocket, place it in the box, and close the little door. "I want to send you another little note, Paw. I still miss you every day."

I want to adopt twin girls. You would love them. Sarah and Susan. Even though they're twins, they are so different. They're each special in their own way. I have a meeting with the administrator at the orphanage tomorrow. She said she has things for me to do. I'm nervous and am

I truly wish he was here, but somehow I know he's still watching over me.

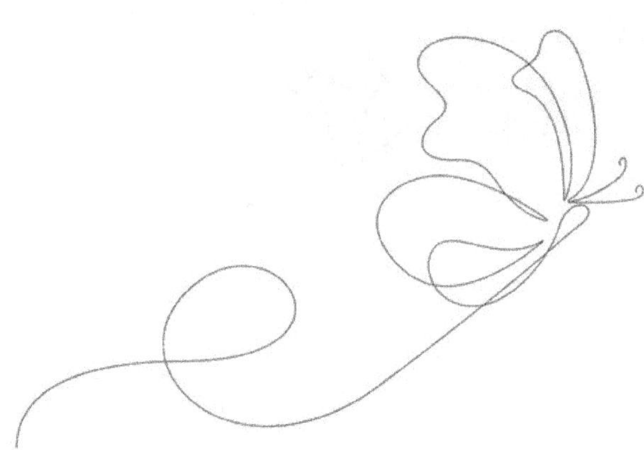

5

My Meeting With Charlie

I sit at my kitchen table with a cup of green tea and honey and make a list of activities I think the children would enjoy between now and New Year's. Since it seems as if time flies so quickly, we are smart to get things organized early. Charlie is good at this. We plan to meet at 6pm.

I jot down ice skating, but realize this may be too difficult for the little ones. So, I erase this and write sledding. We need snow for this and, at this time of year, snow can happen in a day and sometimes we don't get enough snow to sled until after the New Year.

I add hot cocoa with a holiday movie to the list to have with the children after they've had a nutritious meal at some point in this holiday season. Maybe even more than once. I like my cocoa with little marshmallows, and so do the children. Sometimes we even put a squirt of whipping cream on our hot chocolate! YUM!

Thanksgiving is on my list and what I would like to do with the children to encourage thankfulness. Then there's Christmas. I consider the needs of the children and the toys they may want. My goal is to have them make a list of what they want for Christmas. Most of the young children still believe in Santa.

As I look at my ever-growing list, I want to visit Paw before I head over to see Charlie, so I wrap it up and head over. I arrive before the cemetery closes and see I'm the only one there as usual. For a moment, I wonder if the grounds' keeper is the culprit who left the letter, but he doesn't know me at all. In fact, he doesn't know my name. I realize he would see it in my letters if he snooped in Grandpapa's mailbox. Either way, I don't think it's him.

When I open the mailbox, what do my eyes behold? A new paper. I'm excited to see what it says. "Hmm. What do we have here today?" I ask as if someone is standing by to give an answer.

I unfold the paper and read. I look at the tombstone and say, "Grandpapa, I love you and miss you. I wish you could tell me who stopped by and left these two little notes. They are so precious to me. I will keep up with my music and my art. I promise."

I fold the paper and stick it in my jacket pocket for safe-keeping until I get home to put it in my tin treasure box with the other note. Now, I must see Charlie.

I arrive at the orphanage and, at first, I can't find Charlie. I sit in the day room and can hear the children rustling about down the long hallways. After their evening meal, most children stay in their rooms. Some play games with others before bedtime. This is what Charlie told me. He knows their routine because he stays late most days. I never think to ask him where he lives.

I start to doze a little and, suddenly, I feel a tap on my shoulder and hear Charlie softly calling, "Emma."

"Hi, Charlie. I didn't see you when I first came in and decided to sit for a moment. I guess I was more tired than I thought."

"That's ok. Are you sure you're ok to brainstorm this evening?"

"Yes. I'm fine. I'm just relaxed."

I follow Charlie down a hallway I've never been to a large conference room. "I had some hot cocoa made for us, unless you'd like some coffee or tea?" Charlie offers.

"Hot cocoa is fine. It's my fave."

"I know." Charlie pours me a cup and adds a dollop of

whipping cream. "I know you're partial to marshmallows, but I thought it would be a treat tonight to have some whipped cream."

"Thank you. I agree. I like both marshmallows and whipped cream."

"I also have several desserts to choose from. We had leftover cheesecake from dinner with the children and I also have a chocolate cake I picked up earlier."

"I like them both, so you choose."

Charlie decides to give me a little of both. I smile.

"So, what are *you* thinking?" I ask.

"I made a list of some things I thought the children would enjoy doing. First, I wanted to invite you to Thanksgiving dinner. Actually, I think it's going to be more of a lunch. A traditional Thanksgiving dinner, but earlier in the day. This way, the volunteers and cafeteria workers can be free to spend Thanksgiving with their families. Can you come?"

"I would *love* to come. Can I bring something?"

"No. No. We have everything under control. We have the turkeys coming and all the 'fixins,'" he says with a big grin on his face.

"'Fixins,' huh?"

"Well, shucks, Ma'am. My roots go way back yonder, you know," Charlie says in a very thick, unmistakable southern drawl.

"You had me at Ma'am, sir," I return with my not-so-authentic southern voice.

"In any event, you are welcome and invited. We would enjoy having you," Charlie says in his usual and most sincere voice.

"It would mean so much to me to be here with you and the children," I reply. "I actually have some ideas I want to share about Thanksgiving and how the children can participate in a 'being thankful' activity."

"Shoot. I can't wait to hear them," Charlie says as he takes a bite of chocolate cake.

I begin telling him my thoughts in between bites of the delicious cheesecake and chocolate cake.

"I really like your ideas, Emma," Charlie says. "I'll get a large plastic fishbowl to put the 'thankful for' papers in since I don't want the children to hurt themselves should a glass one break."

"You're so thoughtful, Charlie. You take such good care of all these little ones."

"Thank you. It's a great job. I love them all." I can tell he really means it.

"So, I also have some ideas about outdoor activities. At first, I thought ice skating might be nice, but I don't know where we'd get the skates. And I worry it may be too difficult for the young children," I continue.

"Yes, but we can do separate outings if you'd like. The little ones can do something inside, and the older children can try skating or learn to skate. I don't want to leave them out of something fun because the younger children may not keep up," Charlie says.

"I agree. I want to be part of anything you want to do. Also, I thought sledding would be great with hot cocoa-if it snows, of course."

"Yes, *if* it snows." Charlie has lived in Ohio all his life and knows how unpredictable the snow can be. "My mom loved when it snowed. Especially the really pretty snow. You know, the snow that falls lightly and gently covers the ground and all the branches in all the trees. Where there's no wind so a walk in the snow in the full-moon light is magical because the world seems so still. One night, we walked for what seemed like hours, but was really only about twenty minutes. I remember that day like it was yesterday."

"You've never mentioned your family. Is your mom still alive?"

"No. I lost her about three years ago."

"Special?"

"Very."

I saw the look of love for a woman who meant so much

to him, as well as a hint of sorrow for memories that were happy but were mixed with a touch of sorrow as well.

"I'm glad you have such wonderful memories to cherish forever," I say as Charlie nods.

We turn to happy again and continue to go down our list of activities. I get brave and ask, "What do you think about horseback riding?"

"I would have to give it some thought," Charlie replies. "Do you know a stable where they would be safe to ride?"

"Yes. I ride with my friend Evette at a stable where she boards and my old horse lives. They give riding lessons, so they have plenty of calm horses that are safe and won't frighten the children. They would have such a blast. I'm certain of it. I think the horses like the pony-riding days as much as the children do."

"You think so, do you?" Charlie is skeptical, but smiling.

"Yes, sir. I do."

Charlie smiles. We finish our lists-which are pretty similar, surprisingly enough. Charlie and I both have baking cookies, decorating the Christmas tree, making popcorn garland and ornaments, and more on our long lists.

"Oh, I forgot. One more thing. I want each of the children to write a 'wish list' for Christmas."

"A wish list?" Charlie tilts his head.

"A list of gifts they would like under the tree," I clarify.

"That could get a little tricky." He smiles again.

"I know. I'm sure no one will ask for a Porsche or anything crazy."

"No, perhaps not an automobile. But what if they list a pony or a dog?"

"Can we tell them what *can't* go on their list and hope they don't think of something I can't manage. I always say pets don't travel well with Ho Ho on the sled."

"Very funny," Charlie says with a chuckle. "You do think of everything."

"I try. I would like to hear what they would like."

"Sounds good to me," Charlie agrees.

As I get up to leave, I say, "Thank you, Charlie. This has been wonderful. I can't tell you what it means to me that you consider my thoughts and feelings the way you do."

"You make these children's lives better and fun. I always want to hear what you're up to next." Charlie looks at me with his head tilted again and an expression to say, *You always have something up your sleeve.*

"Well, I enjoy them so much. I want to make a difference…"

"And you do," Charlie interrupts me, but I don't mind.

"See you soon," I say. I start walking out of the room.

"Yes. See you soon," Charlie says in a, *Can't wait to see you soon,* tone I may be imagining, but like imagining.

When I arrive home, I change into my comfy clothes and curl up on the couch. I turn on the television for background noise and replay the day in my mind.

A children's author visited the library today. I never think about the authors when I read picture books to the children. I only think of the books I consider wonderful. But this author really inspired me. Her book is about a little boy who is complainy. Is that a word? Complainy? What I mean is, he complains about everything. The oatmeal is too hot, the soap too slippery; there's something wrong with everything. By the end of the story, he has learned to be patient, kind, and wonderful. The illustrations in her book are colorful and downright sweet. She talked about how she was inspired to write her book as she observed her nephew. She reminded me that inspiration is all around us.

A thought comes to me. I think I would like to write a children's picture book. But can I do this? And what would I write about? I think about all the cute and wonderful picture books I've read to the children.

I pick up my journal from the end table and jot down some notes. I need a storyline. Then I need some characters. Do I want to put children in the book or just animals? Children really seem to be thrilled with books with animals.

Alphabet books are a big hit for young readers, but they also like ones about the zoo or a puppy of their own. My thoughts drift, and I wonder why the children at the orphanage can't have pets? It's a natural thing to have a pet when you're young. Not only do they not have their own home and parents, they also don't have pets. *Sort of cheated*, I think.

I once read a book about writing children's books that the standard for picture books is thirty-two pages. How will I fill thirty-two pages?

Do I write it in rhyme or just a small story such as Beatrix Potter's *Peter Rabbit* stories? She wasn't just an author; she was an artist. Her art is what really makes her stories special. I remind myself that I am an artist too!

Grandpapa's note about my art is very encouraging. I can fill a picture book with colorful and cute illustrations the way Beatrix did. I speak of her as if we're best friends who collaborate on stories for children. *Aren't I silly?* I ask myself. Then, I answer myself, *Yes, you're silly*. And that's a silly thing.

Perhaps I'll look over some picture books at work tomorrow. But the problem with this is that it's easy to copy someone else's idea. I want my own original idea. That's going to be the challenge. There seems to be a children's book about everything.

Maybe I can write a book about adoption. Maybe I can make it about how special moms are because they are filled with love, and anyone can be a mom when they love the children they care for.

This idea is something important to me now that I want to adopt Sarah and Susan, so perhaps it would be important to others. I'm not the only woman who wants to adopt children. Many families have adopted children. My thoughts are rambling, as usual.

It's true. I love Sarah and Susan. I have a fun role in their lives now. But, if I adopt them, I would have to set rules. They may not want to live with me. I never asked them. There are so many things to consider. I finally decide love and courage are what guide us and help us be who we want to be.

I keep making notes and fill up six pages in my journal. I'm not sure how to find an artist. Maybe I'll ask Peter if he knows how to find an illustrator. What am I talking about? I will draw the pictures!

As I continue to brainstorm, I'm excited and nervous at the same time to think I could write and illustrate a children's picture book. I should write a letter to Grandpapa about this new idea. So, I do.

Dear Paw, I have an idea to write a children's picture book but you know I don't have the most confidence in myself and feel others do a better job. This never seems to stop me, I realize. I want to write about adopting children and being a mom, even if it's not the traditional way of being a mom. Wish you were here, as always. I decided to draw the pictures for the book. I think I can manage this. I have to come up with an idea for a story that children will like. I know some others think I'm not really a writer, but what do you think? Love, Emma.

I decide I'll take my note to Grandpapa in the morning before meeting Evette to ride. I'm tired, so I pick one of my favorite Christmas movies to watch, curl up on the couch, and quickly fall asleep.

6

Back in the Saddle Again

"It seems like years since I rode Blaze, even though it's only been a couple of months!" I exclaim.

"Isn't it funny how time gets away from us?" Evette asks, but it sounds more like a statement of fact.

"It sure does," I reply. "How's Penny doing for you?"

"She's doing better. I gave her a rest after our accident over the jumps. She isn't lame at all anymore."

"I'm so glad. I was worried."

"Me, too," Evette says with a sigh of relief.

Blaze is my twelve-year-old roan mare, a rescue I couldn't say 'no' to. She doesn't jump, and she isn't keen on being trained to, so I only ride her on the trails.

When I felt I no longer had enough time to care for Blaze properly, she came to live with a friend who needed a child-safe horse for lessons. Blaze is certainly child-safe and has always been a kind and easy horse to ride and to work around. I can't say that about every horse. I donated her with the agreement that I could ride anytime I made time to.

Penny, on the other hand, is a 16.2-hand dark bay thoroughbred mare. 16.2 hands means that she is about five and a half feet tall at the lowest part of the neck, called the withers. A 'hand' is a measurement of four inches. She is as bold and beautiful as her rider and will jump any fence perfectly that Evette points her at.

We tack our horses. In other words, we put their

saddles and bridles on so we can ride. I decide to ride in my western saddle because I'm just in the mood to mix it up today. But I prefer an English bridle and bit because I've never become accustomed to the loose rein in a western bit and bridle. I feel more secure with the English bit and bridle because it has an extra strap that keeps the horse's mouth closed, and this helps me have more contact with the horse's mouth; and, therefore, more control over the horse.

I spray a little bug spray on Blaze and hand the bottle to Evette.

"Ready?" I ask.

"Sure am."

We mount our horses and head for the trail. "Seems you have something on your mind, Emma."

Evette has been my best friend since we were young girls. We met at a stable and have shared our love for horses and riding ever since.

Evette is a stunningly beautiful blonde-haired-blue-eyed woman who is model thin and rides like a princess. She sits in the horse's saddle as if she was born there. I can't help but remember how difficult it was for me to ride when I first started. I bounced a little more than was comfortable on my first pony, Sammy. The bouncing was difficult on the horse's back as well as it gave me a headache to hit the saddle so often and so hard.

Now I think no one would ever know I once struggled to sit comfortably on a horse as I sit my seventeen-hand mare and we walk and trot with ease to the trails behind the stable. All the years of practice have made it much more comfortable for me and the horse.

"I have so many things to tell you," I started. "First, I'm still writing letters to Grandpapa.."

"Of course, you are."

"But the strangest thing happened. I received two letters back in the mailbox."

"Really?" Evette asks with disbelief. "Tell me more."

"Well, I wrote grandpapa and told him how I feel I'm

not much of a musician and how others think I don't play very well…"

"…..and why you only play by yourself…"

"Yes, and I wrote about my art… you know..'

"Like everyone's better than you," Evette finishes my thought."

"Yes, again. But I've never seen anyone else in the graveyard. I've never even seen a worker or anyone preparing sites."

"Who do you think put the notes there?"

I shake my head slightly and shrug. "No idea."

"What did the notes say?" Evette asks.

Suddenly, Blaze seems to know it's time to trot on. We have a special place on the trail where we pick up the pace, and Blaze decides to do so without waiting for me to ask her.

"Emma! Wait for me," Evette calls.

As we ride past all the fall-colored trees, I'm reminded of why I fancy fall in Ohio so much. The changing colors of the leaves are incredible. The burnt orange and yellow, and red, and even the brown leaves are magnificent as they sit on the trees, fall to the ground, and lie scattered over the ground like a crunchy blanket.

The air is slightly cool and pleasant today as the sunshine speckles along the path through the branches and leaves to warm us as we ride. A 'creek' runs alongside the path to guide us. The only sounds we hear in the woods are the birds chattering in the trees and the bubbling of the water beside us. These are a welcome relief from the hustle and bustle of our small town, which is nowhere as congested as the larger cities around us, but still busier than the woods.

After about ten minutes of trotting along, we both say, "Ho," and the horses slow to a walk. It's funny how even if only one of us says, *Ho*, both respond because they know the command.

"That was invigorating!" I'm so happy to be riding. I feel free and forget all my worries when I ride.

"For sure," Evette agrees. "So, tell me about the letters.

I'm dying to know."

"I wrote Paw about the music as I said. I told him I love playing and, even though I'm not as good at it as others, it doesn't bother me, but sometimes I think I should quit playing. I wish he was here, but …you know…"

"And.."

"Well, when I went back to visit, I saw this little white paper in the mailbox and, when I pulled it out and read it, I cried."

"EMMA! I'm at the edge of this saddle. What did it say?"

"You're funny. I love torturing you," I say, smiling.

"You do a VERY good job of it." She is exasperated.

I can hold out no longer. "It said, *Dearest Emma, PLAY, play darling. I love hearing the music and it brightens my day every time I hear you play. Fill the world with music! You don't have to be perfect, you just have to love it and you do! PLAY and play and play.* As I said, I cried."

Evette is speechless for a moment; then asks, "Do you have any idea who sent it?"

We both realize Grandpapa didn't write the note or put it in the mailbox. "I wish he had. I have no idea who did though. And, like I said, I never see anyone in the graveyard. I'm not sure who took the time to read what I sent to Grandpapa and who took the time to write back. Or who knows me so well, for that matter."

"Freaky! Didn't you say you got two notes?" Evette moves her head towards me as if she will be able to hear me better if she does.

"Yes. There was a second note just the other day."

"Do tell…"

"I wrote Grandpapa about my art.."

"And…"

"I told him the same thing I always do-how I feel everyone else is so much better at art than I am."

"You always do that," Evette comments matter-of-factly. "You put yourself down and compare yourself to others. You're a great artist! I put the sunflower picture you painted for me in my living room so *everyone* can see."

"That's what he said!" I'm so surprised to hear her words. "Are YOU the one who wrote the notes?"

"No. What did that note say?"

"It said, *Darling Emma, Never, never, never stop creating your lovely art. I treasure every masterpiece you create. You should never compare yourself to others. You will get discouraged if you try to be like anyone else. Be your wonderful self and get those brushes out and paint! Everyone can create.*"

"That sounds exactly like what I *would* say. Do you have any idea who sent it?" Evette says with a puzzled expression.

"No clue." I sigh. I don't mention that I dropped Grandpapa letters about my wanting to adopt the children and write a children's book.

We walk our horses along the path in silence for a few minutes. Finally, I say, "I know it's not Grandpapa leaving the notes. I'm not crazy."

"Course not."

"Now that I think about it, I did see someone out of the corner of my eye the other day."

"Really. How exciting!" I can see the 'tell-me-all-about-it' look on her face.

"Nothing to tell really. When I looked again, there was no one there. Let's run these girls."

Evette nods, and we both ask our horses to gallop. Galloping is faster than a canter. We cover ground quickly, which makes me feel like the jockey I wanted to be when I was a young girl. I pretend we're at Churchill Downs and it's Derby Day. We're leaping out of the starting gate and running down the stretch! But we're just in the woods along the trails, darting around the bends in the path. My Blaze is ahead of Penny by a neck! Evette has no idea I'm fantasizing about winning our little race.

After fifteen minutes at a fast gallop, we ask our girls to walk again.

"That was great!" Evette exclaims.

"Sure was," I reply.

As we walk along, I say, "I guess we should turn around and head home. What do you think?"

"Guess so. I enjoy our rides and time together. You haven't mentioned Charlie in a while. What's happening with him?"

"Not much. He's such a great guy. He had so much fun the other day with the children. We carved and decorated pumpkins and he made a mess just to help the children have fun."

"Sounds great."

"He is. He talks to me a lot, but it never goes any further. Peter, on the other hand, asked me out for this weekend."

"Are you going?"

"Sure. It's just dinner and a walk."

"Sounds good. You've never mentioned Peter. How do you know him?

"He's a librarian. He works with me."

"Cool."

"Yeah. I have to admit their attention is flattering. They are different though. Charlie is quieter and more comfortable to be around. Peter's wonderful, but I feel as if I always have to be 'at my best' when I'm around him."

"Can't relax, you mean?"

"Yes, I guess that's what I mean. He's nice and he's a great librarian. He often leads story time for me, and he does fun things with the children at the library. He's easy to talk to. He even came to the orphanage and helped with the pumpkin party the other day."

"Interesting. By the way, are those two letters you found in the mailbox the only two?"

"So far. I've written other letters to Grandpapa since then, but I haven't checked the box again.

"What are these letters about?"

"I'll tell you if I get more letters back!" I snap.

We both smile. We walk the horses back to the stable so they can cool-out properly before we return them to their stalls. This helps horses avoid complications such as muscle injuries and colic.

"I wrote and told him how I want to adopt the twins. I also wrote that I want to write a children's book."

Evette doesn't say anything, and I realize most of the day's conversation has been about the letters.

"So, you never talk about what's happening in *your* life, Evette."

"My life is the same. I work at the law firm and ride with you. And that's about it. I read a good book now and then and watch my favorite movies again and again."

"You should come to the orphanage with me sometime."

"I'd love to. I can't wait to see what letters you get about the other letters."

"Hey, what do you think about my bringing the girls for a horseback ride?"

"I think that would be fabulous. Can I help?" Evette is such a great friend.

"It would mean everything to me if you would."

We finish untacking our girls, give them a brief hosing, and then return them to their stalls. I fetch two flakes of hay, one for Penny and one for Blaze.

"Thank you for the ride," I say to Blaze as I pat her neck. This is something my trainers taught me to do a long time ago-always *thank* the horse for the ride.

Just as we leave the barn, I spot a goose walking around the barnyard. "Who's this?" I ask.

"Her name is Gertie. She's a beautiful goose. She sits on eggs that don't hatch. It's sort of sad. She really wants to be a mom. The ducks are moms. She hangs with them."

"How sweet is that!" I think Gertie has given me an idea for my children's book.

We both leave, and I head over to see Grandpapa. Driving seems so odd because I usually walk to the cemetery.

Today is different since I drove to the stable and left from there. I'm anxious to check out the mailbox.

There's no letter back today. My last letter from two days ago and the one I left this morning are still in the box. After I spend an hour talking to Grandpapa about all that has happened in the last few days and how I enjoyed my time riding with Evette, I stand to leave. I walk to my car and, surprisingly, see Charlie walking toward me. I blurt out, "Hey, stranger. What are *you* doing here?"

Initially, Charlie fumbles for words and then says, "I was driving by and saw your car and, when I didn't see you right away, I thought something may be wrong."

He looks relieved when I say, "You really are the most thoughtful and kind person I know, Charlie Parker. How did you get to be so?"

"Aw, shucks, Ma'am," he says in his exaggerated southern manner, "I'm just doing what anyone would do for a lovely lady such as yerself."

We both smile, and I finally say, "Thank you, but I'm just fine. I was riding with Evette, so I drove here from the stable."

"I see."

It doesn't dawn on me to ask Charlie how he came to be driving by, but the orphanage isn't too far from here, so I conclude it's a chance meeting.

"Well, I guess I'll see you tomorrow at Gift of Love?" Charlie says inquisitively.

"Yes. I have a meeting with Mrs. Carter. I also wanted to confirm we're gardening with the children tomorrow."

"Sounds interesting. Tell me more." Charlie speaks as if it's the first he's hearing about gardening.

"About Mrs. Carter or the gardening?" I ask playfully.

"Both."

"Well, we talked about the gardening project for a while and set it for tomorrow. Ring a bell? The children planting flowers around the building and maybe a small tree or two in the yard?"

"Yes. I remember that."

"Great. Are we gardening tomorrow?"

"Yes. Yes, we are. And about Mrs. Carter?"

"She wants to meet with me about adopting Susan and Sarah?"

"I heard something about it."

"Really. What?" I'm a little shocked.

"Word travels. You know that. I was talking with Mrs. Carter one day last week, and she mentioned it. She asked me about you."

"What did you say?" I'm intrigued.

"I said there would be no better home for the twins than with you."

I'm touched. That is the sweetest thing I could imagine anyone saying. But what else would Charlie Parker say?

"Thank you," was all I could muster.

Suddenly, I remember mentioning to Evette about the twins riding horses and blurt out, "Charlie, we talked about riding horses when we met the other day. Do you think I could take Sarah and Susan to the stable to ride one day? I really think they would like riding a horse." I'm almost begging.

"We can talk about it. I think it's a great idea." He smiles.

We leave, and I realize I'm happy he supports my desire to adopt the twins and how I want to take them riding and more. He seems pleased and supportive.

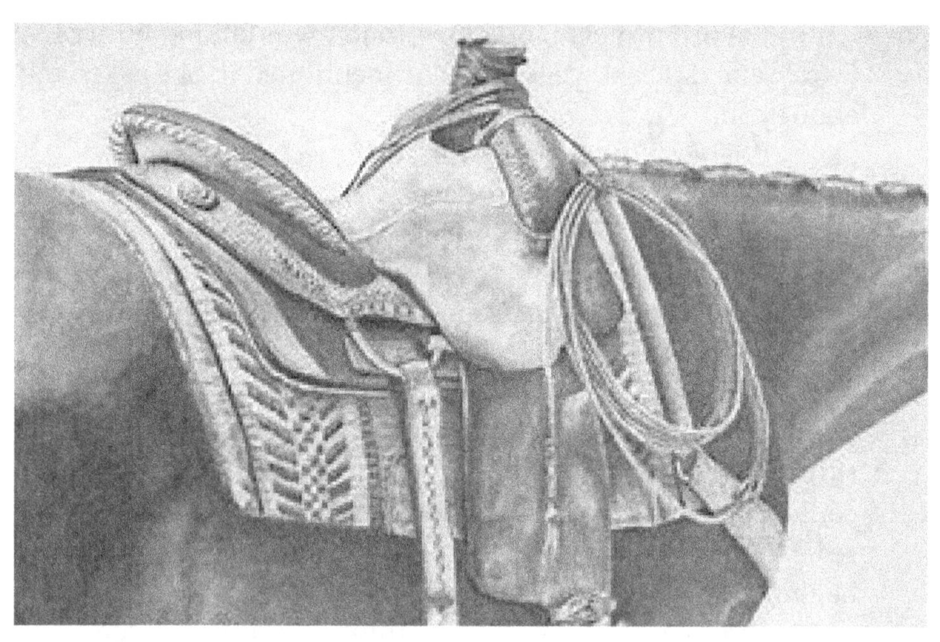

7

The Application and Gardening

After my yet another quick breakfast, I dress in an old pair of jeans and a white t-shirt for gardening with the children. I have gardening earrings that are yellow watering cans. I bought them instantly when I saw them at a nursery one year many years ago. I wear them when I garden at home too. I want to visit Paw before I head to the orphanage. For some reason I want to check the mailbox. I have to admit I'm curious and excited to see if there's another letter.

When I arrive, I find my letters are the only letters in the box. I'm a little disappointed. I like the game of receiving letters back, even if I don't know who's behind them. Maybe it is Evette after all.

I walk drudgingly back to the orphanage for my meeting with Mrs. Carter. At first I was afraid to talk to her, but today I'm ready to get the process underway.

"Good morning, Emma," Mrs. Carter says sweetly as she motions for me to come into her office and take a seat.

"Good morning," I reply.

Charlie enters the room. I'm surprised, but don't say a word.

"Emma, I asked Charlie to join us today," Mrs. Carter says.

"Hello, Emma," Charlie says warmly as he stretches his hand to shake as if we're strangers meeting for the first time.

"Charlie..." I say. I nod as I shake his outstretched

hand limply.

"Well, let's get started," Mrs. Carter begins. "I took the liberty of getting the application for you from Child and Family Services, Emma."

"Thank you," I reply. I take the papers.

"The process can be quite lengthy, and the application is the first step. You can read through the papers and send them to Child and Family Services when you've completed them. If you have any questions, feel free to reach out to me or Charlie."

The only words I can say are, "Thank you."

I'm slightly confused as to why Charlie is with us. Mrs. Carter seems to sense this and says, "Did you know Charlie is the Assistant Administrator here?"

"No... I.... didn't," I say slowly and with great surprise in my voice, "But..." I look at him with my head tilted like he does to me.

Charlie interrupts with, "Yes, and I make a great children's activities assistant as well. Don't you think, Emma?" He smiles.

"For sure." I have had no idea how important his position is here at the orphanage. I'm embarrassed to think of all the times I ordered him around during my time with the children, not to mention the pumpkin party fiasco. Charlie has never reacted in any way but kindly to me.

"I'm going to help facilitate the adoption process as well as Mrs. Carter," Charlie announces.

"I'm g-g-g-grateful," I stammer. I'm still trying to process this newly discovered information.

"In addition to Charlie's involvement, Emma, there will be others participating," Mrs. Carter informs me.

"Oh, like who?" I ask. I'm a little nervous.

"There are counselors who will meet with you as well as inspectors who come to your home to view your living arrangements and its suitability for adoption and raising the girls. They probe into your finances and your work commitments as well as your ability to provide care for the girls and child care when you're working. These things and more."

"I've wanted to ask if my being single impacts their decision to allow me to adopt the girls?" I know I asked this before, but I really need to hear someone say they take it into consideration that I'm single, but consider other things more so.

"That may be an important factor in their decision-making," Mrs. Carter says bluntly. She never sugar-coats anything. Just this once, I could have used some token of encouragement. "But, as I mentioned before, love is the key to adoption. They look at everything."

Sensing my fear, good-ol'-Charlie comes to my rescue, "Emma, if you meet all the requirements, I'm certain they will make the decision you want them too. It's a huge process and you have a few weaknesses, but you have many strengths. Mrs. Carter and I are on your side all the way because we believe you love the girls and all the children here at Gift of Love."

I'm reassured. I can't thank him enough for his kindness. It gives me the courage to thank them both and excuse myself.

"I'll be right out to help with the gardening today, Emma," Charlie says with a smile.

"You don't have to. I never realized you're an assistant administrator."

"I enjoy helping you and I'm going to help you today as well. I know you weren't expecting me to be an administrator, but I haven't changed."

I look into his beautiful and kind hazel eyes. He is wonderful. My heart settles and I say, "I'll see you in the day room."

I walk to the day room where I left the gardening tools along with the flowers and small trees we'll plant today. One of the assistants informs me that the children are finishing their lunch, so it will be a few minutes before they're ready to go outside.

I'm ok with this. I put the application papers in my backpack and continue processing discovering that Charlie's an administrator. What have I been thinking? What else could he be here? He's too smart to be an aide. How did I never know this? Seems to me I never took the time to investigate what his role is here when I'm not here.

I decide to check out the papers Mrs. Carter gave me. There are a lot of them. I take them back out of my backpack. I get nervous again and tell myself I can look them over when I get home. So, I put them back in my backpack. Boy, am I nervous.

After a long five minutes, here come the children! I treasure the moments I hear their laughter and chatter. They try so hard to stay in a line and walk quietly, but it is just too difficult for three to twelve-year-olds to do.

"Hello, children," I say happily.

"Hello, Miss Emma," they say, but not all at once. It's music to my ears.

"Hi, Charlie," I say as I see him enter the room.

"Emma," he nods. I almost laugh because he has changed clothes since our meeting with Mrs. Carter. He's dressed in *farmer* clothes now. I'm not used to seeing him dressed this way. His faded blue, worn overalls hang on him as if he's lost weight I didn't know he needed to. His straw hat is charming, and his black muck boots complete the overall *farmer* look today.

"You look different," I say.

"Ready for planting," he says with a smile. He looks a little out of breath, as if he ran a quick errand before getting started with the planting. "You do know I used to help my mom with her gardening and chores," he adds, as if he needs to explain how he came to have these clothes.

Taking the focus off Charlie's attire, I ask, "Ok, who wants to plant some flowers and trees?"

They all do. They are a rag-tag lot today, dressed in old, torn, and baggy clothes; clothes put aside for activities such as this, where the children are likely to get dirty. Orphans have very few belongings, and the orphanage tries to keep their 'better' clothes in good repair. Today, they're dressed like Charlie. Or maybe Charlie is dressed like them.

"Let's get to work, farmers," I say and chuckle as the children help pick up the flowers. Charlie and the assistants help bring the planting tools.

The younger children choose the chrysanthemums to plant. The older children are given trees because they're a little more challenging to plant.

Charlie has nicely prepared the areas we will be planting these flowers and trees. He removed the grass in a few areas and worked the soil to make the dirt softer for the children to make their small holes to plant their flowers and trees. How thoughtful.

"When did you have time to prepare all this?" I ask.

"An administrator has to do what an administrator has to do," he says with laughter in his voice.

"Are you making a joke of my not realizing how important your position is here when I treated you as if you are a hired hand every time I come?" I had to get it all out.

"No joke. I'm more than happy to help you, Emma. These children are my priority here. You need help, and I want to help, and I have helped, and I will continue to help. Keep bossing me around. I like it."

"Well, I don't think I can do that. I'm going to do my best to make it a collaboration-a joint project every time I come. We're partners if you're still willing to help me. I'm so sorry I didn't know."

"I didn't want you to know until now. I see how you love these children, and your reaction to me and to them is genuine. I don't want that to change."

"You really are special, Charlie."

"I'm glad you think so. I think you're pretty special too, Emma." He winks and we realize the children are running all over the yard. We must get these children working on plants and trees. They have energy to beat the band.

With plants and small trees in tow, we give each child a small trowel shovel just their size. Then, we pick a spot for each child to dig a small hole, place their plant or tree, and then fill in the hole with more dirt. We have small watering cans filled with water so the children can water their plants. The children promise to water their flowers and trees every day. I tell them I will check on this. I assure them we'll have another planting party in the spring with spring flowers.

The older children have larger shovels. Charlie supervises as they dig bigger holes than the younger children, plant their trees, fill the holes with dirt, and generously water the trees with a hose. One of the trees is an apple tree. The other is a pear tree. I'm not quite sure what the third tree is, but we'll see when it bears fruit in the spring. Maybe it'll be a peach tree!

Michael picks up a worm and brings it to me, "Miss Emma, look at the worm…"

"Yes!" I snap. "Very, very nice, Michael, but I think we should put the worm back into the dirt so it can wiggle around there. The dirt is where the worms live."

Michael giggles and places the worm back into the little hole he dug for his flower. He thinks worms are tremendous. I think they are terrifying. I know they are small and just wiggly things, but I don't like them. Thankfully, Michael doesn't realize my feelings and compliantly obeys my request to return the worm to the dirt.

All of a sudden, Jack accidentally sprays Joyce with the hose. "Hey!" she shouts.

Jack doesn't realize he's done this until Joyce takes the hose and sprays him back!

"YEOW!" he cries. "I didn't do it on purpose!"

When the others start laughing at the two of them, Jack takes the hose from Joyce and begins to spray all the children. The little ones think it's fun and play in the dirt that has now turned to mud. The children slosh around and slip and slide in the wet grass and muddy areas.

"Stop!" Charlie has never raised his voice before.

All the children stop immediately, and the hose is shut off. All eyes are on Charlie.

"Please go to your rooms for a change of clothing," Charlie says in a calm and collected voice.

"I'm never going to be allowed to come back," I say in a soft, worried tone.

"It's alright. The children will get cleaned up, and this mess will be sorted out. It's not your fault they had a spray fight."

"Maybe not, but if I hadn't suggested the planting...."

"It's alright. Everything's alright. They had fun, and now they will clean up."

The assistants are efficient at shuffling the children to their rooms and undressing them, cleaning them up, and then dressing them in clean, dry clothes.

They all come to the day room where I'm waiting to see if all is forgiven.

"Everything's fine, Emma," Charlie says.

"I'm so sorry. It seems every time we try to do something, chaos ensues," I say in my *I don't want it to be my fault* voice so I don't get into trouble.

"It's alright. The children would like a story."

I read a children's story about trees and flowers to the orphans as they stretch out on the reading rug. They're tired and a few of them fall asleep. After the story, they head to their rooms for nap time.

"If you need any help with the application, Emma, I'm happy to help," Charlie offers as I start to head out.

"I may take you up on that. I'm a little nervous and don't want to make any mistakes."

"You won't. I think everything's going to be alright." Charlie's confidence is reassuring.

"Thank you, Charlie. And thank you for being so nice to me all the time."

"My pleasure, Emma."

I head home for a small lunch of my own. I place my application papers on the counter and tell myself I'll look at them later.

I head to the cemetery with a short note about my gardening day. My mind wanders back to the events with the children. All in all, it was great fun planting with the children. Yesterday, I planted rows of flowers at Grandpapa's house to brighten up everything. I had a good time digging around the house and putting in the seasonal mums. The impatiens and snapdragons I planted in the spring were slightly droopy, so I remove them, making room for the yellow and white mums. It's nice to do things with the children instead of alone at home. I continue my walk to see Grandpapa.

I wrote him:

> *Dear Paw, this is a short note. I'm a little tired today, but I wanted to write you about the day we had gardening with the children. It was so much fun. I sound like a broken record about feeling like I'm less skilled than everyone else, but it's what I struggle with daily. I think I'm not good at gardening, but I love flowers and want them to blossom and make the home we shared bright and beautiful. I wish you were here to see the mums – as always – and to tell me what to plant. Will write more next time,*
> *Love, Emma*

The park is buzzing again. Today, families are having picnics and have replaced the fun-filled dog show of weeks ago with children racing around picnic tables and eating hot dogs and corn on the cob. The picnic tables are covered with cloths, and food is in baskets, bowls, and on trays. I think, *I wish I knew these folks.*

Everyone is wearing the same shirt that says, "Hudson Family Reunion." Family. How great is that?

I miss Grandpapa and being a family with him. Just the ordinary things I will never have with him again. Coming home and seeing him on the steps. Happy to see me. Our small talks about the day and the neighborhood. Things I once took for granted. Now, when I come home, I still see him there. His crooked smile with few teeth, but a heart filled with goodness and kindness. A simple man with only an eighth-grade education, but the smartest man I ever knew. The man who taught me love and the importance of taking care of family.

I continue trudging along. I'm always excited to visit my Grandpapa. This time, when I open the box to slip in my note, there are two new letters inside. I'm delighted as I reach in and take the letters. As I open the first one and read the words, I slump to the ground next to Paw's site, and the tears flow like a river today. I hold the letter to my chest and softly say, "I hope these words are true, Paw. I hope they are right about adopting the girls." A few tears drop onto the paper. I just hold the paper tighter.

After sobbing for more minutes than I thought I could, I open the second letter. I think, *Yes, I will write my little book.*

After I mull over the words in the letters for what seems a very long time, I say, "Paw, it's Thanksgiving next week. Then Christmas. Our favorite time of the year. I have plans to visit the children for Thanksgiving, but I will be by to see you."

Silence.

Wouldn't it be amazing if the mailbox talked back to me the way the letters came back to me? Sometimes I think silly thoughts. Paw isn't even the one sending the letters. I'm amazed at how nonchalantly I accept these letters that could not possibly be sent by my precious Grandpapa, but I think it's because I believe in my heart these are the words he *would* send to me about adopting Sarah and Susan and writing a children's book if he could. Some moments I want to know who's behind all this, and sometimes I'm content to not know.

For now, I gather my thoughts and pick myself up and make my way back to my warm and cozy home.

8

Thanksgiving

Since I don't really have a family, I'm looking forward to Thanksgiving with the children. 'I hope Charlie's working,' I whisper to myself. Before joining the children for Thanksgiving dinner-lunch really-I decide to hike over to see Grandpapa. I have a letter. It reads :

> *Dear Paw, It's Thanksgiving. I miss you as always and especially on holidays. It's a little lonely without you, but I have been invited to share Thanksgiving at the orphanage. I'm sure there will be turkey and dressing and sweet potatoes - all your faves - and more.*
> *Remember our first Thanksgiving together?*
> *You didn't know how to fix a turkey, so we decided to go out to eat. Two orphans really!! Ha ha, Paw. I want you to know that on the top of my thankful list today, I put YOU there. I also put other things. I wanted to tell you about Charlie. He works with me at the orphanage and he's a really great guy. I know you would like him. I'd better get going, I have lots to do before I get to the orphanage. Thank you for the last notes. I cried. I'm not sure how the letters are coming to me but they mean more than I can say. I know they are exactly what you would say to me.*

When I arrive home, I get ready for Thanksgiving. I dress fancier than my usual work clothes. Today I wear a yellow dress! For this I must shave my legs and put on hose and fancy shoes as well. It's not a huge sacrifice when you're thankful.

My fancy shoes aren't always as comfortable as my walking shoes, but they make me feel like a princess. I put opal post earrings in because opals are my mom's birthstone. And they're my favorite gem for jewelry. *A little make-up never hurt,* I think as I apply mascara to my eyelashes and pink lipstick to my lips. Some soft blue eye shadow, a little blush to liven up my cheekbones, and I'm ready for some turkey.

Since the orphanage invited me, I don't have to do any cooking and they said not to bring anything. So, I just take myself.

When I walk into the cafeteria area at the orphanage, I'm speechless. The tables are decorated with tablecloths that have harvest designs printed on them. There are large safety candles that the children can't topple in the center of each table. They are lit with batteries and emitting the most delicate fragrance of pumpkin spice. Paper fanned-out turkeys are also on each table. The food smells delicious. My mouth waters as I anticipate the many culinary delights we will soon enjoy.

As I stand admiring the room, here come the children! Laughing and talking and pushing a little because they just can't help being so excited to have Thanksgiving today. They all hold a small paper in their hands and are directed by Charlie-who's here and dressed in a suit and tie today. How handsome.

"Alright, children. Put your papers in this bowl," Charlie says as he opens his right arm to show the children the large glass bowl he placed in the room to collect all the 'thanks for' papers he helped the children write.

"This is a great idea," I comment.

"Thank you, Emma," Charlie says. I didn't realize he heard me.

"You look so nice, Charlie," I say a little sheepishly.

"As do you, Emma." Charlie winks. "Ok, children, now take your seats." I blush.

The children calm slightly and slip into their seats. They check out the turkeys and wonder at the candles. These are not items that usually sit on their tables, so they're interested in these more than the food.

The assistants bring bowls filled with mashed potatoes, stuffing, and corn and place them on the table. They also bring platters of rolls and saucers with cranberry sauce. The last thing they bring to each table is a large platter with white and dark meat turkey stacked high on the platters.

"Let's give a quick thanks for the food so we can enjoy it warm," Charlie says.

The children bow their heads and hold their precious little hands together for prayer as Charlie says a short grace and the children all shout, "AMEN!"

I, Charlie, and the other assistants help dish out food to each child.

"Can we sit by you, Miss Emma?" Sarah asks with Susan standing next to her.

"Of course you can," I say with a big smile.

The girls giggle and follow me so they can sit on either side of me. "Let me fill your plates, girls," I say as I begin serving them.

The meal is enchanting. The children are astonishingly well-behaved. Each is dressed in their *best* clothes-clean and neat for hand-me-downs. They try-although unsuccessfully, not to drop food or drinks on their clean dress shirts and blouses. "I spilled my gravy on my shirt," Tony says and shows me.

"That's ok, Tony. It'll wash out. Don't worry," I assure my flustered little guy. I help him clean it as best we can with some water and napkins. He returns to finish his meal.

The room is filled with the buzz of happy children. Again, I wish I could take them all home with me. I love them all with all my heart. Susan and Sarah sit beside me, "I don't like cranberry sauce, Miss Emma," Sarah states.

"Not many people do, Sar," I reply. "But you do like the turkey and stuffing and potatoes, don't you?"

"Yum, yum," Susan says before Sarah has a chance to say...

"Oh, yes, very much," with a smile that spreads across her sweet little face.

"We have dessert to come as well," I remind them.

"What is it?" Joey asks.

"I'm not sure, but I'm sure it will be great, Joey," I tell him.

There is surprisingly little mess. The children keep the food on their plates and, at worst, on the table. We clean a few faces and put the plates in a large plastic bin to be washed later.

"Who's ready for pumpkin pie?" Charlie asks, holding a pie and a can of whipping cream.

"I am. I am," all the children say.

Charlie is so fun. He loves the children and enjoys seeing them have a great time as much as I do. I can tell. The assistants and Charlie and I place a small plate with a piece of pumpkin pie in front of each child. Then, each table is given a few cans of whipping cream the children invert and push the top to smother their pie with. It's cute to watch them trying to be 'big' as they spray the whipping cream over their pies and then themselves, and a little on each other.

"Whoa!" Charlie snaps. "Let's help a little with this," he continues as we all grab the cans and skillfully finish adding the whipped cream to the pies.

"That was so much fun," Tommy says. He has whipped cream all over his mouth because he inverted the can to his mouth and sprayed. We know he did this because the evidence is present.

"You look like you're having so much fun, Tommy," one of the assistants says before I can comment.

"We're going to have to do a lot of cleaning up," I say.

"There are lots of assistants today, Emma, so it won't be that difficult," I hear Charlie say as I realize he's standing behind me.

After our pie and everyone is stuffed, we head to the reading circle.

"We're going to have each one of you come to the Thanksgiving bowl and pick out a paper to read-or have someone read for you-to share all the things we are thankful for today," Charlie says, leading the group today.

"Can I go first?" Eileen asks.

"Yes, you may, Eileen," Charlie answers and helps her to the bowl.

Eileen places her little arm in the large plastic bowl and rustles around until she decides on a paper to bring out. "I can't read yet," she says as she hands Charlie the paper.

"Let's see," Charlie muses. "It says, *I'm thankful for Thanksgiving Day*. That's a great thing to be thankful for. Thank you, Eileen. You can be seated again. Who wants to be next?"

"I do," Billy, Tony, and Crystal say at once.

"One at a time," Charlie says. "How about Crystal first, then Billy, then Tony?"

Crystal walks to the bowl, reaches in, and pulls out another paper. "I'm thankful for all my friends here," she reads from the paper. "I'm thankful for my friends too," she adds.

"Friends are a great thing to be thankful for," Charlie says sweetly. 'Next," he says.

The others take turns reading from the papers in the bowl. The children are thankful for their toys, snacks, and for their rooms and that Christmas is coming soon.

Then, Sarah and Susan ask if they can read what they wrote because they forgot to place their notes in the bowl. "Yes, you may read yours, girls," I say as Charlie nods.

"We're thankful for you, Emma. We love you and wish you could stay here with us every day. We miss you when you go away."

I'm so choked up I can barely talk. When I look over at Charlie, he's standing there looking at me with a warm smile on his face. "I wish I could too, girls," is all I can manage to say. I take them in my arms and give them a big hug. I can't tell them my plans because I don't want to disappoint them if I'm not granted the adoption.

"We all love you, Miss Emma," George says, and all the children agree.

It couldn't have been a better Thanksgiving. I must tell Grandpapa all about it.

9

The Date

Peter asked me out and I said, *Yes*. I haven't been on a date in a long time. I think this is a date. It may just be friends getting together. I don't know.

As I stand in front of the mirror, I say, "It doesn't matter if we're just friends. I'm happy to have a night out."

I fiddle with my makeup bag and decide on blue eye shadow and the same pink lipstick I always wear. "Blush always helps me look perky," I say slowly as I pat blush on my cheeks.

Tonight isn't a fancy occasion, so casual works. Peter sees me every day and knows what I look like, so my good jeans will do. I top my jeans with my nicest blouse, though - a red silk one. I add my pearl necklace and I'm done.

Then I wait. I read gardening and food magazines to pass the time until Peter arrives.

I jump up from my chair when I hear the knock at the door. I'm relieved when I open the door and find Peter dressed casually in jeans and a nice shirt as well.

"You look nice, Emma," he says, smiling.

"Thanks. So do you."

I grab my purse and keys and lock the door behind me. We walk to his yellow Volkswagen parked at the curb. I love his little 'bug' and have always wanted one. "Love your car," I say.

"Me too," Peter says as he opens my door. I slip into my seat and he walks around to his side. "Where would you like to go?" he asks thoughtfully as he slips behind the wheel.

"It doesn't matter to me, but I was hoping you might be in the mood for pizza."

"You must be reading my mind," Peter says. "Pizza is my favorite. Pizza it is."

I'm grateful he's a cautious driver. Since my accident, I don't passenger well. It was a frightening incident when I lost control on the ice and totaled my small car. I almost died in the crash. I hit my head on the steering wheel and required plastic surgery to close the large gash to my forehead and right eyebrow. Since then, I'm scared when drivers drive too close to other cars or faster than I think is safe.

"Here we are," Peter says as he pulls into the parking lot of the pizza restaurant.

"Thank you for being a careful driver," I say to him.

Peter seems surprised at my comment. "Doesn't everyone drive carefully?" he asks.

"No," is all I say.

We sit at a booth by the front window. This is the seat I like the best because I can see the people in the restaurant as well as the ones walking by. I like people-watching. And it reminds me of times I spent in restaurants with Grandpapa.

"What do you like on your pizza?" Peter asks.

"Well, I don't like anchovies, but I like everything else."

"Don't worry about that. I don't like them either. I usually order sausage and mushrooms. How about you?"

"Sounds perfect," I say. It's easy being with Peter. He's kind. Conversation is easy with him too.

We order and continue talking. "I have some ideas for the library," Peter says.

"Yeah? Like what?" I'm curious.

"Well, I think we could have a theme each week. For instance, one week we can focus on animals in Africa and display books for the children. We can decorate the library like a jungle. Then, another week, we can feature creatures under the sea. We can decorate like we're underwater. Maybe we can show a short movie. What do you think?"

"I think these are fabulous ideas. How long have you been

thinking about them?"

"Not long. I saw what you do at the orphanage. At the pumpkin party, Charlie filled me in a little about the crafts you do."

"Charlie, eh?" I have a crooked smile on my face when Peter mentions him.

"Yes, Charlie. Does he help you every time you go to the orphanage?"

I stopped to think for a moment. "Yes. Yes, he helps every time. I didn't know he's an administrator until recently. I was sort of shocked to be honest. I give him orders and he just follows them. Technically, he should be giving me orders."

"That's kind of funny when you think about it," Peter says, half chuckling.

"I didn't think it was so funny when I found out. I'm embarrassed."

"Why? He seems to enjoy helping. He did with the pumpkins anyway."

"Yes. He's always patient and understanding with the kids. Now he's involved in my adoption process." I don't mean for this to slip.

"Adoption? Who are you adopting?" Peter is as surprised as he is inquisitive.

"Well, it's not a sure thing," I say in a joking tone, "I'm thinking of adopting the twins, Sarah and Susan."

"I admire you for taking on so much responsibility. I'm not sure I'll ever have children," Peter says matter-of-factly.

Surprised, I blurt out, "But you're a children's librarian! I just assumed you love children."

"I do love children. But the children at the library are *someone else's*. I can spend time with them, read to them, and help them find books, and then they go home with their parents."

I can't believe my ears. I'm stunned. My mouth drops open.

"You're surprised?" Peter asks.

"Well, sort of. I understand that wanting children is a personal decision. I just thought you were the kind of man who would settle down and have some, that's all. You're so wonderful with the children."

"I'm not ruling it out. I just know I'm not ready for anything like that right now."

Our pizza arrives. Peter separates the pieces and graciously slides a piece onto a plate and sets it in front of me. "Thank you," I say softly.

"My pleasure, Emma. I can't wait to dig in. I'm starved."

Just as I'm about to take my first bite, Charlie walks in. What are the odds? For some reason, I hope he doesn't see me. No such luck. He turns his head and looks right in our direction. Then, to make things worse, he nonchalantly walks over and says, "Hey, you guys, here for pizza?"

In between bites, I say, "Nice seeing you, Charlie. What are you doing here?"

"Getting a pizza to go."

"Yes. What am I thinking?" I know I'm stammering. We're both stating the obvious. A million thoughts go through my head about what he must be thinking.

"It's nice to see you again, Peter," Charlie says.

"You too, man. Looks as if you got all that pumpkin cleaned up," Peter says in a jovial voice.

"Yeah. It came off pretty easily. Are you guys here discussing work?" Charlie seems a bit concerned about what this is between Peter and me.

"No, we're just having a night out," Peter volunteers before I can downplay our date-if it *is* a date.

"Peter and I are discussing plans for the library. We both like pizza and thought it would be nice to chat over dinner," I say, trying to let Charlie know it's not what it looks like, even though it *is* what it looks like. *Why do I care so much?*

"Well, I'll let you get back to what you were doing," Charlie says as he semi-salutes and walks to pick up the pizza the clerk announces is ready.

"See you Monday at Gift of Love," I say as he walks away.

"See you then, Emma." Charlie leaves without looking back at me.

"Funny running into him, huh?" Peter says between bites.

"Yes. It is funny running into him. I usually only see him at the orphanage, although I did see him the other day at the cemetery and now here. He gets around. If I were paranoid, I'd think he was following me."

"Just a coincidence, really," Peter says. But how does he know?

I'm still shocked about Peter not wanting children. I'm quiet for the rest of our meal.

"How about a short walk?" Peter asks as he sets his napkin on the table, indicating he's finished.

"I'm a little tired, especially after eating three slices of pizza. I was so hungry I surprised myself. I think I'd like to call it a night."

"I get it. You really do like pizza. I can eat four pieces, but I never see girls eat more than two."

"Two is usually my limit, but I was really hungry, like I said."

Peter pays, and we leave the restaurant. He opens my car door again, and we drive home. "You're quiet all of a sudden, Emma. Is something wrong?"

"No. I'm just tired. I'm thinking of all the things I have to do this weekend. I think your new ideas for the library are great. When can we talk about them more?"

"Anytime. We can brainstorm at work next week."

We arrive at my house, say goodbye, and I rush to my paper and pen. I must tell Grandpapa.

Dear Paw, It's me again!! I went for pizza with Peter and found out he doesn't even know if he wants children. I don't think I can consider getting close to someone like this and am glad I found out before I agreed to go out with him again. And, to make matters worse, Charlie showed up. I was so embarrassed to be seen with Peter. I stammered as I tried to decide what to say. He looked hurt. I didn't know what to do. He loves the children at the orphanage like they're his own. It's obvious in the easy way he interacts with them. Peter seems to have an interest in me, I don't think I can go any further with him because

*even though we have some things in common, our goals are
very different when it comes to the children. Especially the
children at the orphanage. Love, Emma*

It's early still. I tell myself I can make it to the cemetery, but
it's almost dark. Maybe I should wait until tomorrow. I decide to
take my letter before work in the morning.

10

Adoption Papers and Gertie

I sit at my desk at the library tapping my pencil; it's a slow day. Luckily, and surprisingly, I made it to work on time. I was sure I'd be late since I hurried to drop my letter to Grandpapa. I've been visiting Paw more often these days and I know it's because I want to see if there are letters for me.

I welcome the slow time at the library. I'm going to catch up on some things and squeeze in a little writing *Gertie* time. The older children are back in school after their Thanksgiving break. I'm sure they're all looking forward to Christmas break.

I want to work on my picture book about Gertie but, instead, I decide to sort through the lengthy adoption papers. When I get to the pages asking me to list references, I panic. I call Charlie.

"Charlie here," he answers.

"Charlie, it's me." I talk quickly.

"Emma, how are......"

"Panicked!" I say before he's finished asking me.

"What's wrong? How can I help?"

I'm comforted by his calm response and willingness to help. I take a deep breath and say, "I'm tackling the adoption papers and am asked for personal references. I don't really know anyone except you. Can I list you as a reference?"

"You sure can. I would love to give you a reference." Have I mentioned how kind and adorable Charlie is?

I take a deep breath and give a sigh of relief. "Thank you. I have to have five references. One down, four to go."

"Who else would you consider using as a reference?" Charlie is determined to get me through this process.

"Oh, yeah. I just remembered, I have Evette and Jan. We've been friends forever. Do friends count? I can also ask my boss. Do you think she's a good reference?" I asked, rambling. I'm so discombobulated I can't even think straight.

"Who, your boss or Evette and Jan?"

"All three."

"I don't know Evette or Jan, but I think your boss would be great. She can let them know you have a good job and are a hard worker. This will help. She can comment on your character and work with the children at your library."

"You're right!" I'm feeling a little better. I still need one more reference.

"There is someone else you may consider asking," Charlie offers.

"Who?"

"I think Mrs. Carter would be willing to give you a positive reference. She has made comments about how wonderful you are with the children. She knows how committed you are to coming to Gift of Love and taking time to do so many things with the children. And, Mrs. Carter happened to hear what the twins and all the children said at Thanksgiving. Plus, it's her desire that each child would have a home of their own. Don't get me wrong, she dearly cares for them here, but understands any child would prefer a home of their own."

"I sure did when Grandpapa stepped in and cared for me."

"What do you mean?" I realize I never told Charlie about my Grandpapa.

"I'm basically an orphan myself," I say as if it's the most natural thing in the world.

"Is that so? Do tell." In my mind I can see Charlie relaxing back in his chair in his office and putting his feet on his desk.

"I lost both my parents in a car accident and Grandpapa took me in."

"That's some long story," Charlie says with a chuckle.

"Sorry, I was expecting more of a story. Anyway, how old were you?"

"About ....seven," I say, fishing for the right age in my mind. It seemed I was always with Grandpapa, so the age frame is slow to come.

"That's young for sure. That's why you write letters to him?"

"How do you know?" I ask. I must say things about my letters to Grandpapa without realizing I'm doing so.

"You mention it more often than you realize. I think it's endearing," he says sincerely.

"I feel connected to him when I write. That's why I put the mailbox in the cemetery. I don't remember telling you," I say, still trying to remember telling Charlie about Grandpapa.

"It was when we first met. You came to Gift of Love asking if you could do projects and activities and story time with the children. You didn't realize I'm an administrator and..."

"You didn't mention it either." I finish his sentence.

"Sorry for that. That seems to upset you."

"Well, I would not have asked you to help. And I certainly wouldn't boss you around the way I feel like I do."

It was Charlie's turn to interrupt me, "But I *enjoy* helping and you're not bossy, you just direct the activity. I tell you this, and you don't believe me. I work here because I *love* the children. I see how much you do too. That's why...." Then Charlie stammered for the right words.

"That's why, what?" I insist.

"That's why I help," he says with a sigh. I know he meant to say something else.

"Thanks, Charlie. I have to go. I see a child who needs my help. I'll be in touch about the papers and be over to ask Mrs. Carter for her reference."

"Sounds great," Charlie says.

We hang up, and I get to work. "How are you, today," I ask the little red-haired girl.

"I'm Harvest," she says proudly.

"I'm Emma. Your name is pretty, Harvest."

Ignoring my compliment, Harvest continues, "I would like

a book about a kitty. I like kitties."

"Let's see what we can find," I say as I take her by the hand to the rows of picture books on the low shelf in the picture book section.

I find a book about the many cats and kitties a little girl sees in her neighborhood. "How about this?" I show her the book.

"Okay," she says.

We sit and look at the pictures and I read some of the words.

"Mama," Harvest says as she looks up and sees her mother come into the children's section.

"I didn't know where she went. Thanks for watching her," her exasperated mother says.

"It's okay. We're in the business of finding something for wandering children to do," I say with a small laugh.

After they leave, I fill out the remaining pages of the adoption form. They ask everything. What you like, what you don't like, how much money you make, where you work and for how long, where you live and for how long, and more.

The most difficult question for me is *why* I want to adopt. Isn't it obvious? I don't know how to put into words that I love these girls and know what it's like to be without parents. I don't want them to be in the orphanage forever. I'll have to think about what I want to write. This is the most important question.

"Looks like you've been busy with those papers," Peter comments on the obvious .

"Yes. These are the adoption papers. They ask for a ton of information," I reply.

"I admire you for wanting to adopt the twins. They're very lucky." Peter says it like he means it. "And, what's this?"

"It's my notes for a little book I'm working on. But I have to go right now. I was only able to stay for a moment at Grandpapa's this morning and, after all this paperwork, I'd prefer to spend my lunch time there." I sweep the adoption papers from my desk, put them in my bag, throw my coat on, and head for the door. I leave my notes for my Gertie story and sketch pad on my desk.

"See you after lunch." Peter's voice trails as I rush out the door. Peter picks up my sketches and the partial lines on my notepad. "Looks interesting," he says to no one in particular.

When I get to Grandpapa, I notice several papers in the mailbox. "Now what do we have here?" I confess, I'm excited.

These papers are light yellow, but the handwriting is the same as the others. It seems a little more scribbled today. As I read, I cannot believe my eyes. I just put my letter about my date with Peter in the box this morning. *Who is writing me?* I wonder. I admit I'm as frustrated as I am excited, but these notes are as lovely as the others and warm my heart. I'm glad someone-whoever they are-is writing me and saying just what I need to hear about gardening and writing and dating and Thanksgiving.

At work, I continue writing lines for my picture book!

How do I make it special and cute? I ask myself. I want to keep Gertie's name since she's the goose I saw at the stable. *Mother Gertie* is the title I mull over in my mind. I like this.

I need some sketch ideas. Let me see what I can find, I say to myself as I comb the shelves in the art section for samples of geese and ducks. I finally come across a book with ideal pictures of geese and ducks for my book. The goose in the art book I like best is the one that looks like Mother Goose. She's white with a long neck and orange beak. She has a peach colored bonnet on and splashes in the pond for a bath. These sketches will help me make my Gertie.

I return to my desk and take out my sketch book. I draw Gertie. I draw her sitting on her big goose eggs. These sketches of Gertie make it easier to see her as I write.

I write my first sentences :

Gertie wanted to be a mom too
That's all she ever really wanted to do

As I'm drawing a little bonnet on Gertie, I hear, "Whacha up to?" It's Peter looking over my shoulder.

"It's my picture book," I reply.

"That's cool. What's it about?" He pretends he didn't

peek.

"Well, don't laugh, but I'm writing a story about a goose who wants to be a mommy but her eggs don't hatch…"

"Sounds a little sad," he interrupts.

"Let me finish. Her eggs don't hatch, but the ducks' eggs do and she adopts them as her own. Or at least she helps be a mommy to them along with the two mother ducks."

"Sounds interesting. And why do you want to write a book like this?"

"Well, when I was at the stable the other day, I saw a goose being a mom to ducks and you know I want to adopt the twins at the orphanage and…" I drift off and then continue, "Writing a children's picture book is a little tougher than I thought. I thought picture books were simple to put into words, but a lot goes into them. And I'm drawing the illustrations too. This is my Gertie." I show him my sketches.

"Very nice. I like the bonnet. I'll leave you to it. If you need me, I'm here."

I appreciate his offer, but want to polish my first lines. So, I start with :

> *Gertie wanted to be a mom too*
> *That's all she ever wanted to do*
>
> *Gertie sat on big goose eggs, hoping for some goslings*
> *She knew they would be the cutest little things*

I look up to see a youngster coming towards my desk. I turn over my yellow pad, "May I help you, young man?"

"Yes. My teacher said I need to pick a book to read and write a report about."

"Do you know what you would like to read and write about?" I ask.

"Not really."

"Let's go to the young readers' section and find something. Are you about eight years old?"

"Yes."

"What do you usually like to read about?"

"I like books about sports," he replies.

"Most young men do. We have several different series to choose from."

I walk him to the section with the biographies of many athletes. "Do you like one sport more than another?" I ask.

"I like baseball. I know all about the players, and I want to be a baseball player one day."

"What's your name?"

"Billie."

"Well, Billie, I'm Emma. Here are some fascinating books to choose from. They tell the stories of many talented baseball players."

I show him books about Babe Ruth, Micky Mantle, Joe DiMaggio, and more. He's excited and looks over all the books.

"If you need more help, I'm right at my desk."

"Thank you," Billie says politely.

It's been a long time since I thought about baseball. I played center field on a girls' Little League team and batted pretty fairly. I also spent time going to professional games in downtown Cleveland. I'd buy a ticket for the cheap seats and then sneak over behind home plate because there weren't many fans in those days.

I return to my desk to see Peter looking over my little story. "This is cute," he says, smiling.

"I'm glad you like it," I say as I take it from him.

"I took the liberty of adding a few lines." He chuckles.

"You did?" I ask, slightly perturbed.

"Well, I didn't think you'd mind a little help."

He leaves and, as I look at what he added, I'm shocked at how much I like it :

Gertie wanted to be a mom too
That's all she ever wanted to do

Gertie sat on big goose eggs, hoping for some goslings
She knew they would be the cutest little things

Gertie says it doesn't matter who you are or what you do
As long as you have love in your heart, you can be a mom too

"I'm surprised, Peter. These lines are endearing and fit the story perfectly," I say to him across the room. "I mean it. These lines are so sweet. You really understand the story."

"Glad to help." He blushes.

I sit with my paper. Maybe I misjudged him. After all, he *is* a children's librarian.

"There's more work to do on this," I mutter to myself.

"Would be happy to help more if you want," Peter chimes into my thoughts.

"What you added is fabulous, Peter, but I'm okay. If I get stuck, I'll let you know."

"Of course." Peter sounds dejected.

I should have let him help, but I write more lines and finally finish the story. I decide to call the book *Mother Gertie*. I add *Mother Gertie: A Mother Goose* to capitalize on *Mother Goose*.

Mother Gertie – A Mother Goose

Goose Gertie wanted to be a mom too
Watching over her own chicks is all
she wanted to do

Gertie made a nest and sat on big goose
eggs for days
In hopes to hatch little ones to love
in motherly ways

Gertie waited and waited hoping for some goslings
She knew they would be the cutest little things

But Gertie babies did not come
Even though she did so want some

*One sunny morning, with a soft little quack
Came a yellow and black duckling – the
first of the pack*

*Then along came four beautiful others
And, suddenly, the ducklings had three mothers*

*Those five little ducklings took to Gertie Goose
They followed her everywhere – there were five ducklings
on the loose!*

*With playful delight, they all went everywhere
Through tall, wild grass – always in Gertie's care*

*And the babies rely on Gertie's protection
For geese are skilled at danger detection*

*Gertie stays close by and watches the
ducklings each day
She makes sure they are safe in every way*

*Gertie leads the entire duckling parade
What a great mommy Gertie has made!*

*Gertie's so happy, now it's easy to see
She has five little duckling babies*

*The ducklings love Gertie likes she's
their own mother
They all know they belong to each other*

*Under Gertie's wing, daily, they
learnt something new
And with every soft quack, their bond
grew and grew*

Gertie and the ducks are a blended

family and full of cheer
In their loving world, they hold each other dear

For family comes in many different ways
And Goose Gertie has found great joy in her days -

She longed for babies and has them now
She really doesn't mind how

Gertie says it doesn't matter who you
are or what you do
As long as you have love in your heart,
you can be a mom too

I tap my pencil on the yellow pad as I look over the story. With all the scribbles, it's a little difficult to see the final version of the story. *I'll rewrite it tomorrow,* I think to myself.

I draw a few more sketches of Gertie with her five little ones and her helping them bathe and play safely.

I'm in a hurry to leave because it's getting late and I want to visit Grandpapa one more time before the cemetery closes. I leave the drawings and yellow pad with the story on my desk.

When I get home, I warm up some cabbage soup I made a couple of days ago. "Cabbage is so good for you," everyone who is anyone says so. I added small potatoes, carrots, peas, onions, garlic, and tomatoes. All my faves.

I keep thinking about my Gertie book. I must tell Grandpapa. I can't wait until tomorrow, so I jot a small note, bundle up, and head to the cemetery. Three trips in one day to see Grandpapa is a lot, even for me. But I have so much to tell him. And, I don't admit it, but I want to check the box. Then, I realize I haven't put any new notes in. I'm a little too anxious sometimes.

The wind whips briskly through my hair and chills my whole body today. I wrap my coat tightly around me. I have a sweater under my coat for extra warmth. A warm headband covers my ears. *I just need something to cover my forehead*, I think as I trudge to see Grandpapa. I must tell him about my Gertie story.

Dear Paw, I wrote a little story about a goose who couldn't have any goslings of her own. She has so much love in her heart though and she ends up helping the duck mothers raise their five little ducklings. I know you'd like it. When I get it finished, I'll bring it and read it to you. I'm not much of a writer but I think I'm almost a writer! Ha ha. You always tell me I'm too critical of myself, but I don't think I want anyone else to see it. At work, Peter saw it. He added a few lines for me. I'm drawing the illustrations. Love, Emma.

At home, I realize I left my little story and the pictures I drew on my desk, but I remember my little story, so I draw a few more pictures for *Mother Gertie* and fall asleep with my pencil in hand.

11

Dance Class

I'm up early today so I can sketch a few more pictures for *Mother Gertie*. I can't believe I'm almost done with the art. The pictures are coming out better than I expected, if I do say so myself. I gather my story pad and other illustrations and stuff them in my backpack. I think projects come easier for me when I enjoy them the way I'm enjoying this little book. Now I have other plans.

Once a month, I join my friend, Jan, for dance class. In the past, I had more time, so I joined her weekly. Jan reminds me of our dance date every month. She's a fabulous dancer. I can't say enough about her graceful movements. They are fluid and just plain gorgeous. It's as if she's floating over the dance floor. She's a true artist moving her body flawlessly.

On the other hand, there's me. The girl who loves things she will never be *great* at, but I refuse to stop trying and stop loving dancing. I give it my best effort each time I hit the dance mat. My return letters say, I need to stop comparing myself to others. A friend once reminded me 'comparisons are odious.' This means they are horrible, loathsome, detestable-all things bad.

The reason comparisons are such is because no one is quite like someone else. Everyone is unique and has different levels of talent. Everyone needs to celebrate themselves and learn to accept themselves with all the good and not-so-good things. A goal I set is to do better about not comparing myself to others. I have a lot of work to do. I need to stop comparing.

I wrote Paw about *almost being a dancer*–no surprise I realize – but this was long before I started receiving notes, so I never read words encouraging me to *dance like no one is watching and enjoy every moment*. I'm sure Paw would have said these things to me. He never said a discouraging word.

Today, we're doing a combination of ballet and modern dance. Since neither of us toe-dances, we do more modern dance. I pretend I'm a talented prima ballerina, but it truly is pretending. We started dancing many years ago, and Jan has progressed. I just enjoy the exercise and getting together.

Jan is extremely thin and has long, dark brown hair she ties up in a small bun when she dances. Her black leotard and tights fit her like a glove. She moves her arms around as if to wave away cobwebs throughout the room. She leaps and twirls and makes me look like a two-left-footed klutz. Just as everyone else, Jan reminds me I'm *way* too hard on myself.

Even though I doubt myself at times, I love to dance. It's elegant and I do it semi-privately. The girls we dance with have known us for many years. They aren't judgmental and never comment on my lower-level talent and failure to progress in my dance talent. They merely dance around me. I watch closely and try to imitate.

Dancing isn't only great exercise, it helps maintain balance should one experience balance issues. Today, we're dancing to Swan Lake music. The ballerinas in the group toe-dance with graceful movements around the room. Jan and I tiptoe on the front balls of our feet to move around the room like the professional dancers who dance the ballet.

After class, as we get ready to shower. We decide we're going to our favorite pie restaurant for dessert. I call it the pie restaurant because we only get pie there. They have sixteen different pies and we've tried them all.

"I think I'll get the brownie pie with vanilla ice cream tonight," I say, smacking my lips.

"Sounds like you'll just break even with the dance today and the brownie and ice cream," Jan comments.

"You mean calories?" I ask but don't wait for an answer

as I add, "You worry about calories, I know, but I treat myself once in a while. It's not like I splurge every day." I'm trying to justify my unhealthy choices.

"That's what you say to yourself?" Jan asks as if she's Sherlock Holmes investigating a big story. She has her towel in her arm and her soap in her hand.

"Yes. That's *what I tell myself*. I deserve something nice for the work I just put in dancing. Breaking news, 'Emma eats pie!'" I say flippantly. I turn and head to the shower.

Jan follows and we change the subject. As the water flows all over my tired, perspired body, I wash my hair tonight as well.

"I met someone last week," Jan informs me matter-of-factly.

"Do tell," I say. "You sound pretty casual about it. Is he nice? Handsome? What does he do for a living…?"

"I'll tell you everything. Just one question at a time."

Jan takes a minute to gather her thoughts and heads into the empty shower stall next to me. "He's pretty much a computer genius. He works from home. He's handsome enough. He has brown hair and the most gorgeous blue eyes. The thing I like best about him is how he treats me. He's the kind of guy who opens doors and pulls out chairs. He took me to a fancy restaurant and I felt a little out of place, but we had a nice time."

"Wow! I'm so glad for you. Obviously you're seeing him again?"

"For sure." Jan takes a breath and continues, "Just when you think you're never going to find someone, you do."

"That's when they say it works out best." Suddenly, Charlie comes to mind.

"How about you, Emma. Are you seeing anyone?"

"No. I had a date the other night with a fellow librarian."

"Peter?"

"Yes. I forgot you know all about my life."

"Yes, I do. And how did that go?"

"It was nice. We like a lot of the same things. But I don't think he's someone I could build a life with."

"Oh. Why not?" Jan peaks over the shower stall with a

tell-me-everything look on her face.

"He came to the orphanage with me to help with a pumpkin party…"

"And…. what about the date?"

"Well. It was great until he said he doesn't think he wants children, at least not right now. When I mentioned adopting the twins, he implied he could never adopt a child. He said he may want children someday, but not really sure if or when. You know how much I want to adopt Sarah and Susan. I could take all those children home to be completely honest."

"I know you could," Jan says sympathetically. "You do have a lot of love to give, and you should adopt them."

"It's strange about Peter. He wrote the most endearing lines to my *Gertie* story. He wrote like someone who should have children."

"What *Gertie* story?"

"Oh, sorry. I'm writing and illustrating a children's picture book about a goose named Gertie who adopts the ducklings in the barnyard as her own."

"Sounds great!" Jan exclaims.

"Anyway, as far as the adoption goes, I have to muddle my way through all the paperwork and interviews and such. By the way, I put you and Evette down as references. Is that okay?"

"Sure. Would be very happy to give you a reference. Have you told the girls yet?" Jan asks.

"No. I don't want them to be disappointed if I'm not granted the adoption. That would be difficult for them. I just keep going to the orphanage doing story time and activities."

"Evette tells me you've been getting letters *back* in Grandpa's mailbox."

"She's not supposed to tell…" I start to say.

"It's only me, Emma."

"I know."

"Do you have any idea who's writing and putting them in your Grandpa's mailbox?" she asks.

"No. I like getting them, but sometimes it freaks me out that someone knows me so well that they answer them exactly the way I think Paw would. But, to be honest, I like getting them. I find myself rushing to the cemetery to see if there's a new letter every chance I get."

"You said 'you like getting them' twice," Jan comments.

"I did. I like getting them. There. That's three times." I laugh. Jan ignores me.

"Are there new letters?" Jan asks a lot of questions.

"I told Paw all about Peter and how I was upset he didn't think he wanted children or could adopt a child. He works with children all day. I just took it for granted he would want a child-any child. He said he thinks about having children, but as I said, he's not sure when or about it at all."

"Did you receive a letter back?"

"Yes. It was short and said, *Always trust your heart, Emma. You will know when the right person comes into your life.*"

"Wow! Is that the only one?"

"No. I wrote Grandpapa about gardening and feeling that many plants don't live in my garden. I wrote how I wanted to brighten up the home we shared and make it beautiful. This fall I planted mums. The letter back said, *Having a green thumb takes time. Keep planting and enjoying beautiful flowers. I love it when you do. They brighten up my world, too.* Freaky, huh?"

"Amazing."

" Do you know who's putting them in the mailbox?" I ask like I'm interrogating her.

"No. Not a clue." Jan sounds truthful.

"Is it Evette?" I ask sheepishly.

"I don't think so. She didn't let on like it was her. She had the same reaction we have to the letters."

"Well, I don't know how to figure out who's behind the letters back, but someday I guess I'll know." I stop and contemplate whether I really want to know. Then, I remember, "Oh yeah, I wrote about writing a children's picture book…"

"How's the book coming along? Tell me more about it." Jan is sincerely impressed.

"I'm almost done, actually. I have a couple more illustrations to finish. The lines are done. Like I started to say before, it's about a goose who wants to be a mom but none of her eggs hatch. The ducks hatch five eggs, so Gertie helps and is mom to them along with the duck mommies."

"Well, how appropriate is that for my best friend?" Jan smiles, and my heart feels her approval. "Did you write Grandpa about this?"

"Of course," I say smugly.

"And…"

"This morning, when I visited Grandpapa before dance class, I found a letter in the mailbox that said I write great notes to Grandpapa. The note also said he's proud of me and I'm not *almost* a writer, I *am* a writer!"

"I concur!" Jan says, almost shouting.

"Thank you. I'm having fun drawing the illustrations as well."

"That's fabulous. Your art is precious. I've always loved your work. I just wonder who's sending those notes."

"Until we find out, let's get some pie!"

We dress and head to the restaurant. When we arrive, Evette is already there and has saved us a booth. "Over here," she waves. "How are you? How was dance?"

"I'm good," I started, "Jan is a magnificent dancer."

"This I know," Evette says, smiling at Jan.

"Thanks, girls. It's great to spend time with my besties," Jan says, trying to take the focus off herself.

"I've been looking forward to pie all day," I say as I get comfortable.

"Me too." Evette doesn't have calorie concerns either. We know Jan is watching her calories, so we don't say anything about the calories to her.

We look over the menu and, as planned, I order my warm brownie pie with vanilla ice cream. The combination of the warm pie with the cold ice cream is one of my very favorite things. We chatter about life and love and then we talk about my letters.

"How are you going to figure out who's sending the letters?" Evette asks, a little concerned.

"I don't know. Sometimes I want to know and sometimes

I don't. I just don't want them to stop. I guess deep down inside I wish they *were* from my dear grandfather. I miss him so much. No one told me grief is forever. How do you stop missing the ones you love and lose?"

We sit silently for a moment. My friends know I have more to say; I just need a moment.

"I thought about putting up one of those hunting cameras, you know, the ones they put in trees to watch for animals."

"I've heard of those," Jan says.

"I wanted to ask the groundskeeper if he ever sees anyone near Paw's grave…."

"That's a good idea. We have a mystery on our hands," Evette says, wringing her hands together as if she's solving a sci-fi mystery.

"You guys…" I start to say.

"We only want to help," Evette says.

"I know. Someday I'll figure it out. I know they'll stop when I find out who's leaving them. That's why I'm not in any hurry. It's not one of you two, is it?" I ask, pointing at both Jan and Evette.

"Not us," they say together.

I'm not sure I'm convinced. These are the only two girls in the world who know everything about me. They know what Paw would say and they have heard me doubt myself my whole life. In any event, we finish at the restaurant, say *goodbye,* and go our own ways; until we get together again.

12

Bess and the Interview

Today's a big day. A case worker from the adoption agency is coming to see my home and interview me. This is the next step after reviewing my references. I think this is a good sign.

I'm not sure they were supposed to, but Evette and Jan showed me the papers the agency sent them. I was happy to see all the nice things they had to say about me. It's good to have friends.

They wrote things like I was someone who would love the girls as if they were my own and give them a warm and loving family. They added that I take care of my home and am committed to my work as a librarian. They see me often, and I'm always in good spirits and generous with my words of encouragement to them as friends.

I don't have the courage to ask Charlie or Mrs. Carter how they filled out the reference paperwork.

After I submitted *my* papers, I spent days fixing up the spare room for the girls. It took me at least half an hour to pick out just the right color of soft yellow paint for the walls. Then, I added a wallpaper border near the ceiling filled with elephants, giraffes, and tigers. I had a fun time making *my* little girls' room.

I bought two twin white sleigh beds with matching vanities. On the vanities, I placed small brushes and hand mirrors. I added ring dishes and necklace holders, knowing we will shop for these things when they came to live with me.

Each girl will have her own dresser. They don't have many clothes to bring from the orphanage, but we'll soon fill the drawers with clothes they can choose for themselves. I couldn't resist Disney-character lamps to place on each dresser.

I also found small, round, ceramic night lights that cast images of stars all over the room when lit. I know the girls will be enamored with them and want them on all night.

I found sheets with kittens playing with balls of string on them and pillowcases to match. I also bought stuffed heart-shaped pillows and put one on each of their pillows. I ordered personalized wooden name plaques with poems about how special they are and hung them on the wall over their beds.

I cleaned the house like never before and strategically placed healthy snacks of apple sauce and yogurt in the fridge. I hid all my unhealthy snacks and vow to eat healthier when the girls are here.

The paperwork the agency sent thoughtfully prepared me for my interview by including a checklist of ways to make the house childproof. I look over the list and tell myself, *I think I've covered everything*. I put in outlet covers, moved all the cleaning supplies to higher cabinets that the girls can't reach, bought a fire extinguisher for the kitchen, put fresh batteries in the smoke detectors, and did about twenty-three other things to make the house safe.

With an hour to spare before the case worker arrives, I head to the cemetery for a talk with Paw. I'm so nervous, I can't sit still at home. As I walk past the park, I spot a small, brown dog with large white and black spots - some sort of beagle mix, maybe - limping around the park. One of her paws is swollen.

"Hey, little girl. Come here. You can trust me," I say softly, trying to reassure her.

She slips under a picnic table and, when I get close, she runs out from under the table to the swing-set area. I slowly follow. I remember I have a small package of cookies in my backpack. I take a cookie out and show it to her.

I see she's hungrier than she is frightened. When she approaches, I give her the cookie. She eats it quickly, then comes looking for more. "I have more of those for you," I tell her. She's less afraid, and I give her another cookie.

"Do you belong to someone?" I ask as I look around the park. I don't see anyone who appears to be searching for her. I gently pat her neck and check for a tag.

BESS is the name on her collar. "There looks like there's a phone number…" I say, trying to decipher the number. "We'll call when we get home."

It never occurs to me to leave her here alone, especially when she appears to be hurt.

"I'm on my way to see my Grandpapa. Would you like to come with me?"

I stand up and begin walking, looking back at her over my shoulder. She follows. I walk slowly and keep a close eye on her because there's traffic on this street and I don't want her hurt worse.

She follows me all the way to Paw's grave and sits like a lady as I place my letter in his mailbox. "I suppose you'd like another cookie?" She seems to know what I'm saying because she stands to take the cookie and wags her tail.

My letter to Grandpapa tells him about the inspection today and how Evette and Jan said such nice things about me. "I want you to meet Bess," I say to Paw. Then I look at Bess and say, "Bess, meet the greatest Grandpapa in the whole world." She wags her tail and nudges my backpack for another cookie.

"We don't have much time today, Bess. I've got to get home. I need to take you with me, but I need to make sure you don't run into the street. I think I have something to tie to your collar…." I mumble as I search my backpack and pull out a ball of yarn I put in there for a craft project with the children. "Here we go."

I measure six strands of yarn into five-foot lengths and tie them in knots along the length of the strands to make the leash strong. Then, I make a loop at both ends and tie the strands around the collar at one end and hold the other end as a make-shift leash. "I sure hope you walk well on a leash. Let's see," I say to her as I gently begin leading her home. I decide it will help if I show her the cookie she'll get when we get to our destination.

Bess walks - or should I say limps - home with me easier than I expected after it took me that short while to gain her confidence in the park.

She steps into the house as though she's lived with me forever. *It's nice to have a dog*, I muse. "I don't have any dog food, so these cookies will have to hold you for a while. Let's put a bowl of water down for you. I have an important interview today. I need to call the number on your collar and then I'll take a look at that paw of yours." I ramble when I'm nervous. And today I'm nervous.

I call the number and an elderly man answers, "Hello."

"Hello. My name is Emma. I found a small dog in the park. Her collar has your number on it. Is Bess your dog?"

"Yes. She is!" He exclaims. "You found her?"

"I did. Her paw seems swollen, but she's okay otherwise." I don't want a stranger to come to my home, so I ask, "Where do you live? I can bring her to you a little later. I have an important appointment soon."

He tells me he lives a few blocks away and he's homebound. His caretaker took Bess for a walk and didn't come home with her. "I've been so worried."

"I can imagine," I say. "I can bring her over, but I'm expecting someone to come to my home to inspect it for me to adopt two girls from the Gift of Love orphanage." I don't know why I'm telling him this. Nervousness about the inspection may be making me uncharacteristically chatty. Or, I'm just losing my mind. Either theory is plausible.

"That sounds wonderful. I'll be here whenever you can come," he says thoughtfully.

"I'll ring you when I'm on my way."

"Okay," he says as I hear a knock on the door.

"I've got to go. Call you soon."

I open the door to find a stocky woman who's shorter than I am in a khaki-colored business suit under a black winter coat. She's wearing horned-rimmed glasses perched halfway down her nose. She's holding an electronic tablet and tapping her foot as if I took too long to open the door.

"I'm Ms. O'Brien from the adoption agency," she says, surprisingly warmly.

"Please come in," I say, inviting her in. "Welcome to my home." I try to shake off my nervousness. "Can I get you something? A cup of tea? Hot cocoa? I'm sorry I don't have coffee. I don't drink it…"

"Nothing for me, thank you," she interrupts. "I'm here to see your home and talk about you."

I begin, "It was my Grandfather's house. I lived with him. He left it to me in his will. Where would you like to start? We can sit in the front room." I'm rambling. I stop talking and show her the way to my living room. I let her tell me what to do next.

My home looks like a Christmas museum filled with decorations that have been passed down in my family for three generations. Christmas lights are strung above the kitchen cabinets. Tiny wreaths that were crocheted by my grandmother hang from the cabinet knobs. Paper mache, snow-covered houses and a church sit on the mantel. She stops to admire my snowman collection and Christmas trees - my ceramic ones and my large decorated one. "I love Christmas too," she says with a smile.

"It's my favorite time of year. Grandpapa, I mean my Grandfather, let me decorate the whole house every Christmas. Here are pictures of my Grandpapa and Grandmama. And these are my parents," I say as I pick up photos from atop the piano to show her.

"Lovely," she says. She sits on my couch and opens her tablet. She moves her index finger across the screen and asks, "How long have you lived here?" She looks up with sincere interest.

"Almost all my life, really. I came here to live with my

grandfather when I was quite young. My parents died in a car accident."

She doesn't comment on my loss or my arrangement with Grandpapa. I'm not sure if that's a good sign or a bad sign. It's probably no sign at all. I need to relax.

"Do you have a mortgage? What are your monthly bills?"

"There's no mortgage. My Grandfather gave me the home and everything in it. I haven't changed it much, just the room I've prepared for the girls. I have a good job and no debts. I have just the usual bills: electric, water, and such."

"I see it says here," she says as she scrolls through the pages on her electronic tablet, "you're a librarian."

"Yes. I'm the head children's librarian, actually. I love my job. It's close to home…" I stammer slightly. I'm sure she knows how much money I make each year because I put it on the paperwork I filled out.

"May I see where the girls will stay?" She changes the course of our conversation.

"Yes, of course. I can show you the whole house."

"No need. Just the girls' room."

I lead Ms. O'Brien down a short hall to the girls' room. "Their bedroom is next to mine, so I will be able to hear them if they call out in the night. I've prepared everything in anticipation of their coming to live with me." I decide to be optimistic. I know the room is darling by anyone's standards.

Ms. O'Brien walks around the room and looks at everything. "Each girl has their own bed. They'll appreciate that. And your choice of room color is soft and happy," she continues. "The border is cute, too. They'll like these little lamps that cast scattered light over the room…"

"Those are my favorite things too," I add.

She opens the top drawer of one of the dressers and sees socks and pajamas. "You've been shopping," she says.

"I have." Suddenly, I'm embarrassed. Isn't this something someone wanting to adopt two girls would do? I hold my breath, hoping to change gears again.

"I see they don't have a bathroom of their own," she comments.

I'm not sure how to field this comment, but I say, "No. We'll share the bathroom at the end of the hall." I show her the only bathroom in the house. "It's an older home," I say, trying to apologize for not having a separate bathroom for the girls.

"There were five of us growing up with one bathroom in a house not much smaller than this one," Ms. O'Brien says, smiling as if remembering sibling skirmishes.

Ms. O'Brien notices Bess has been quietly following us from room to room. "You have a dog?" she asks.

"No. I found this lost dog in the park today. I contacted the owner and am taking her to him after our meeting. Do you mind if people have pets when they apply to adopt children?"

"No. Not at all. As long as there aren't any allergies. I think I've seen enough," she says and taps her tablet one final time. "We'll be in touch."

"Can I ask if I'm a suitable candidate for adoption? I have my heart set on these girls coming here and…"

"I can't tell you if you'll be granted an adoption. It's not for me to decide. The board makes that decision. You and your home are lovely. Your references are solid. We'll be in touch," she says again and turns to leave. I follow her to the door and watch her walk to her car.

I sit with Bess for a moment. "Looks like I have some waiting to do, Bess," I say as if she can make everything turn out all right. She just looks at me and wags her tail.

I put my coat on and reattach the makeshift leash I made for Bess. The address her owner gave me is just a few blocks away. "Come on, girl. Let's go home to your daddy. I bet he's been worried sick about you."

When I knock on his door, a handsome gentleman opens and exclaims, "Bess. My dear Bess," and stoops to continue, "Where have you been? I was so afraid I'd never see you again. What happened to your paw?"

He ignores me for a few moments as he reacquaints

himself with his pet. "I think she's going to be okay," I say. "Her paw seems better just in the little time I've spent with her."

"Oh, I'm sorry. I was so caught up with Bess, I forgot you were standing there."

"It's okay. I understand. I'm Emma. Bess is a sweet dog."

"She sure is. She's a lot of company for me."

"I may consider getting a dog soon. I've applied to adopt two young girls." I repeat myself a lot these days.

"I think every child needs a pet," he says. I agree with him.

I turn to leave, wish him well, and head home to mull over my time with Ms. O'Brien.

13

Sledding, A Tree, and Hot Cocoa

When I wake and look out the window of my bedroom, I can't believe my eyes! It snowed! Hurriedly, I pick up my phone and call, "Charlie!"

"Yes, Emma?"

"It snowed!" I exclaim.

"I see," Charlie answers. He knows he drives me crazy when I'm so excited and he's so calm.

"Can we go sledding this afternoon? Then pick out a tree for the lobby. And then come back to the orphanage for hot cocoa and maybe watch a Christmas movie or decorate the tree and dayroom? Maybe some cookie baking? Oh! And the children need to write their wish lists for Ho Ho!"

"Slow down, young Emma," Charlie says in his *old man* voice. "That's an awful lot to do in one day. I think we can manage the sledding, tree, and hot cocoa. Let me get some things together and get back to you."

"Ok," I say, still excited. I want to do *everything*.

I hang up and gather my sledding clothes and sled in anticipation that we will sled today! My sledding clothes consist of flannel-lined snow pants that are very warm. Also, I pick a bulky sweater to wear under my waterproof jacket and decide to take my newly purchased knit hat and mittens.

After putting out my clothes, I grab three cookie sheets and pack microwave popcorn. I search for and find my child-safe needles and string to make popcorn garland. "Charlie said he has all the ornaments for the tree," I say to myself, semi-relieved.

I'm so excited! One would think it was the first time I ever went sledding. I look at the lists Charlie and I made of things to do. I'm happy sledding is possible since-did I mention-it snowed!! There are three feet of soft, fluffy snow covering the ground, and I know the perfect hill to sled down.

While waiting for Charlie's call, I take a few minutes to finish my last two illustrations for *Mother Gertie*. I add the words to the pictures and put everything in a folder marked, *Mother Gertie*. I'm organized because I know myself too well. Sometimes I put things in places I can't find them when I need to. I want all my *Gertie* material together in one folder.

RING! I answer, "What's the verdict?"

"We can sled and then pick out a tree. The kitchen staff is preparing the hot cocoa and will put it in thermoses for the kids." Charlie has it all worked out.

"Yeah! I have to stop at the library for a moment and then I'll be right over," I say and hang up.

I dress, grab a donut, and walk to the library with my sled in tow, my full backpack, and my precious *Gertie* folder.

"Peter, I want to go sledding with the children today. Is this okay with you? Can you cover for me?"

"Sure. Have a nice time," Peter replies without looking up from a book he's browsing through about bridges.

I have a few moments before I need to leave, so I skim through my folder with my *Gertie* notes and pictures. I put the pages in order and look over the words and pictures quickly. I'm pleased.

I make copies of my work on *Gertie* and put one copy in my backpack and leave the other copy in a folder on my desk for safekeeping until I return from sledding. I always make copies of things I create just in case I misplace pages.

Then, I walk to the orphanage, dragging my sled behind me and toting my backpack with the cookie sheets, popcorn, string, and needles. I also threw in one of my favorite Christmas movies, *The Magic of Christmas.*

When I arrive, the assistants have the children dressed and lined up. They look so cute in their bulky coats and stocking hats. Their boots are on almost all the correct feet. I'm sure it was a huge undertaking having seventeen children ready for an outing. They're perfect for about thirteen-point-four seconds. Then, they're children again-laughing and talking and fidgeting. The staff loads sleds and extra clothing for the children, anticipating wet clothing.

"Now, you older children must, and I *mean must,* watch over the younger ones," Charlie says kindly but firmly.

"We will," Annette replies. She is the oldest child at the orphanage and always helps with the young children.

"Thank you, Annette," Charlie says, more relaxed. "Ok, let's get on the bus."

We lead the children single file to the bus and they all climb on. They're excited too and talk all at once.

"Let's sing a song," I suggest to help with the bedlam. "How about *Jingle Bells*?"

"YEAH!" the children chime in.

I stand at the front of the bus and lead the children in Jingle Bells, Jingle Bells, Jingle all the way…This helps them focus and not push others off their seats.

I smile as I think they're so cute with their own thermos and a small sack lunch the kitchen staff sent them off with.

Annette helps keep the young children in their seats as promised. "You have to wait until we get to the hill, Tony," she says as she closes his thermos. "And no snacks until lunch time."

Young children are impatient. It's part of being young. I understand this because I'm still impatient. I can't wait to get to the hill and begin our special day out.

When we arrive, we split the children up into groups of three younger ones with an adult or an older child. Annette takes three children. Will takes four children. Mary takes three children and Tina takes three children. This leaves me with Sarah and Susan. Charlie joins us at the top of the hill.

"Where's your sled, Charlie?" I ask. I'm just now noticing he came sledding with no sled.

"I was hoping to hitch a ride with you, Sarah, and Susan."

"YEAH! Mr. Charlie's going down the hill with us!" Sarah and Susan say together.

"Well, I guess that's that," I submit.

We help the others put the children on their sleds and watch them glide down the hill, happily shrieking as they quickly descend the hill. There aren't any trees on the hill so we're not concerned they may be hurt.

"Ready?" I ask Charlie.

"Yes. Let's do it," Charlie says as he lifts Sarah onto the sled. Then he takes Susan and places her behind Sarah. "Your seat," he says as he shows me where I will sit on the sled.

"Thank you, Mr. Charlie," I say in a slightly mocking tone.

"Very funny, Miss Emma. I'll sit behind you."

"I'm glad I brought my big sled," I say as I sit behind Susan and put my arms around her little waist. "Put your arms around Sarah," I say.

"Here I come," Charlie sits behind me and places his hands on my waist. This is something new. A slight shiver comes over me. "Here we go!" Charlie exclaims as he pushes us off the top of the hill. We begin sliding quickly down the hill.

It feels like a mountain as we glide along the freshly fallen snow. My stomach is thrilled like when I ride a roller coaster. The cold wind whips across our faces, especially across Susan and Sarah's since they're in the front of the sled.

When we reach the bottom, our sled topples over and Saran and Susan are dumped into the snow. "Let's make angels, Sar" Susan says.

"Yeah, Suze. Let's," Sarah agrees.

The girls plop on their backs and begin moving their arms and legs to make snow angels. "Very nice, girls," I say. "Do you want to sled the hill again?"

"Yes, we do!" they both exclaim.

Thoughtfully, Charlie pulls the sled up the hill with one hand while he carries Susan in his other arm. I carry Sarah.

A few of the boys try to make snowballs, but the snow is too fluffy. They throw the snow in the air and stand under it, make-believing they're being snowed on. "Look at us, Miss Emma!" They giggle as they play.

The children have fun going down the hill. They don't mind trudging up to do it all over again. We sled until the little ones are chilled - about twenty-five minutes.

When we get on the bus, as anticipated, the children are a little wet and feeling the cold now. Charlie, Annette, the other assistants, and I help remove wet clothing from the younger children. We're glad we thought ahead and brought extra dry coats, gloves, and mittens for them.

"Let's have our hot cocoa," I say. We help the children grab their thermoses and everyone enjoys the cocoa. It's just the right temperature to drink safely. Tony spills a little on his coat. "It's ok, Tony. I'll help you clean it up," I offer.

As I wipe the cocoa from his coat, Joey asks, "Can we eat our lunch?"

The older children and assistants help everyone on the bus. The children cutely open their sack lunches on their laps. Peanut butter and jelly again. We have this often because it's the easiest sandwich to travel with. The staff packed apple slices and a small snack cake as well. Everyone finishes their lunches and hot cocoa, and we're off to our next stop.

"Who wants to get a Christmas tree?" Charlie asks.

All the children shout, "I do. I do. I want to get a Christmas tree."

What Charlie didn't say is that a tree was already picked out and waiting for us at the tree lot to save time.

We pull up to the tree lot and park. The children walk around the lot looking at the different trees. They see fir and hemlock and spruce trees. "Which tree is best, Miss Emma?" Tina asks.

"They're all nice, aren't they?" I respond. "I think it's whatever one *you* like best is the best."

"I like this one, Matthew says, pointing to the largest spruce on the lot.

"That's a beautiful tree. Sure is *big*," I say.

"I like this one," Joey says as he points to a small crooked little tree.

"What about this?" Sarah asks about showing me a beautiful, smaller, but fully branched, fir tree.

"I love that, but we have to ask Charlie," I say.

Then, Charlie says, "How about this one? It's tall and has *big, fat, full* branches for all our ornaments." He doesn't mention it's the tree he already picked. He wanted the children to have fun looking at the trees.

The children agree to take Charlie's tree home. The tree-lot attendant helps Charlie secure our tree to the top of the bus. *It's quite large*, I think. *Thankfully, not as big as Matthew's favorite tree.*

When we arrive back at the orphanage, the children are shuffled to their rooms to change from their outdoor clothes into casual clothes for crafting, decorating, and baking. No one minds if these clothes get messy.

"That was so much fun," I say to Charlie.

"Yes. It was. It's worth the extra effort to take the children somewhere and watch them have fun."

Charlie recruits a man from the maintenance staff to take the tree from the bus and gently place it in a stand Charlie prepared in the dayroom. Scattered around the tree are boxes filled with ornaments collected over the years.

"You thought of everything," I say to Charlie.

"We made lists, remember."

"Yes, but it is incredible how organized you are."

"Well, I wanted to pack in as much as we could in one day. You wanted to do so many things, it's the only way I could think to make it happen."

"Thank you," I say. I'm overcome by warm feelings for him. *I wonder how he feels?*

There's no time for these sentimental thoughts. The children run into the day room. As I begin to unpack my supplies, my *Gertie* papers fall to the floor. "What's this?" Charlie asks as he helps pick up the papers.

"Nothing, really. I wrote a children's book, and these are copies of my illustrations and story for the book."

"These are marvelous. You really are a talented artist," Charlie says sincerely as he looks at the pages.

"Thank you. I didn't mean for anyone to see the book; I wrote it for myself."

"No. No. You should publish this. These pictures are very good. Your story's about a goose?"

"It's about adoption. Gertie is a goose who can't have her own goslings, so she adopts the ducks' babies."

"Sounds really cute." I never heard Charlie use the word 'cute' before.

"I like it. I just played with the idea." I pack up the papers and change the conversation to our next activity. "So, where do you want me? I can help with popcorn garland or decorating the tree…"

Charlie agrees to change the subject away from my book, "How about you work on the wish lists for Santa, or Ho Ho as you call him. I'll help with the popcorn and decorating with Josie. The kitchen staff will help the children bake cookies. There. I think everything's covered."

"Sounds good." I'm relieved. I think about Charlie liking my *Gertie* book. To be honest, I didn't think anyone would like my story or illustrations. But I always doubt myself. I really only wrote it for personal reasons about my own life and wanting Sarah and Susan and to be a mom.

Time to stop thinking about myself and Gertie. I gather a few children to a small table in the day room and say, "What I would like you to do is make a list of things you want Santa to bring you for Christmas. If you can't write, I'll write your list for you."

"What do we write?" Angela asks.

"You tell me or write what toys or clothes or whatever

gifts you would like for Christmas."

"Anything we want?" Tony asks.

"Well, Santa may not be able to bring *everything*, but he will try. Don't put animals on the list because Ho Ho has a difficult time bringing them on the sleigh," I say. I also know pets are not permitted at the orphanage.

The children who can write begin writing their list. I'm surprised to see Tony wants a stuffed bear because he's such a rough and tumble little boy. But he also wants a big fire truck to use to rescue those in need.

Lisa wants a doll and a small stroller to take her places. The others make modest lists with various items ranging from a baking oven to Barbie clothes. After they finish their lists, we rotate the children.

After about an hour, all the children have completed their Christmas lists and the cookies are baked. They smell delicious. I didn't have much for lunch, so the kids and I *sample* some chocolate chip and oatmeal raisin cookies.

The tree is partially decorated with the most beautiful ornaments I have ever seen. There are tiny wreaths and reindeer ornaments as well as photos of the children in popsicle frames. The popcorn garland became more of a snack for the children than a decoration for the tree.

"How about a movie?" I ask.

The children are excited to see *The Magic of Christmas*. They curl up on small bean bag chairs or cushions on the floor. I put the movie in. After about eight minutes, Charlie and I see that all our children are sleeping. They've had a very big day. We decide the movie will have to wait until another activity day.

I help pick up the smaller children and take them to their beds for a nap before their supper. "You don't have to do this, Emma. We have staff to help," Charlie says, meaning to be thoughtful.

"It's not work to me, Charlie. It's part of being with the children and helping everyone."

He lets me continue helping and then I leave for home.

I have so much to tell Grandpapa.

When I arrive home, I make a small supper of spinach and cheese ravioli with marinara sauce. I take my pad and begin to jot down my note. I tell Paw how much fun I had with the children, and how I spent time with Charlie, and how he put his hands on my waist down the hill. I wish this day never had to end. I tell Paw how lonely the house feels without him or anyone here but me. Sometimes I feel more at home at the orphanage because there are so many people there. I include that I think I have feelings for Charlie and wonder if he could ever have feelings for me. I sign, Love Emma and fold my note. I lay it on the counter to take in the morning before work. I'm so tired, sleep comes quickly.

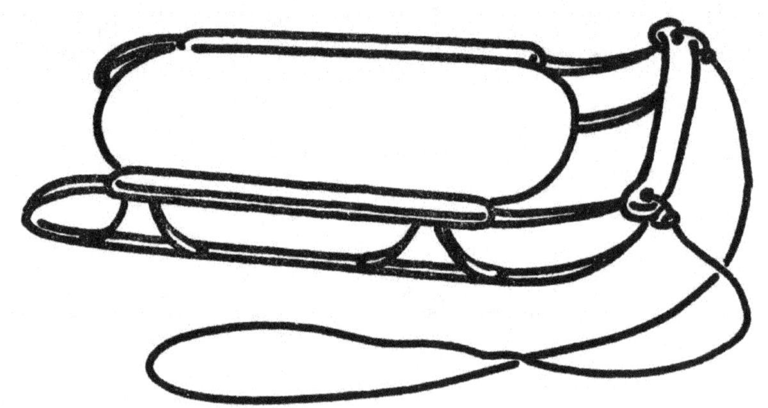

14

Donations

I stuff the children's lists and sizes in my oversized purse and I'm off to bring all these needs and wants to the donors. I dislike referring to my behavior as begging, but I guess that's okay as long as the children benefit from my efforts.

Since I don't have a red suit with a black buckle and red hat, I dress in navy cotton pants with a white shirt and pink-laced sweater. I have flat black shoes that I wear with my nylon socks. I wear my hair up with a small clip. I think it makes me look more 'business-like.'

I think a little make-up will help me look more professional, so I put on my usual light-blue eye shadow, a touch of blush that's barely noticeable but highlights my cheeks, and my favorite rose-colored lipstick. I have a cashmere black coat that I save for special occasions. I think this is a special occasion.

As I slip into my driver's seat, I start the car and let it warm up. I'm happy. The generosity of others warms my heart in a way I'm unable to express. I realize these companies are successful and affluent, but their gifts are voluntary and generous.

My first stop is the clothing store. As I walk through the door, I am smitten with all the new winter clothing on display. The blue and white bulky Nordic-looking ski sweaters are my favorite. They look so comfy and cozy, like something you'd wear huddled in front of a fire at a ski lodge with, you guessed it, hot cocoa. Not that I ski. The one and only time I tried to ski, I thought my life was over.

I donned the skis alright and tried to get the hang of skiing on the baby hill. My friend gave me an unofficial ski lesson, and I thought I could manage an actual hill. So, I jumped on the lift. But, when my friend and I arrived at the top of the mountain, I didn't know how to exit the lift and turn in the direction down the hill, so I almost went down the opposite side of the hill right off the lift! Scary moment because the trees haven't been removed from that side of the mountain, so I would have collided with one of them.

In any event, I managed to position myself correctly to ski the hill, but had no idea how to ski. I should have stayed on the baby hill and practiced the 'pizza' thing they all told me to do with my skis to slow me down the hill. This is where you turn your feet inward to make the ski tips touch in a 'pizza-piece' shape.

Truth be told, I didn't sail down the hill because when I began going faster, I slipped down to my bottom and slid down the hill on my fanny. I didn't try a second time. But I did enjoy dressing for the fun.

In the store, I also pass by various hat, scarf, and glove sets. These are more of my favorite things. Today, I cruise the counter and pick up a white set. The soft white knit scarf and gloves are *so* white and *so* soft. I take time to adore them and think they are the most beautiful things I have seen in a long time. Then, I pick up the matching hat. I put it over my head and look in the mirror on the counter. *It fits me perfectly*, I think to myself.

Then, I check out the red set. Another of my favorite colors. White and red things go together in my mind, even though these two colors seem so different. White is conservative and goes with everything. Red is bold and must coordinate with my other clothes. I think the red matches my black coat. As I slip my hand into the red mitten, I'm amazed at how soft it is and how it fits so perfectly, just as the white set did.

As I admire the mitten on my hand, the sales clerk

appears, "Is there something I can help you with today?" she asks in a slightly perturbed manner. I guess they only want customers to try on things they plan to buy.

"I was just admiring these beautiful sets. I'm going to think about it some more. Thanks anyway." I pull the mitten off my hand and place it back on the counter.

If they don't want people to admire them, why do they have them on the counter? I ask myself. One day I'll treat myself to a set, but today isn't about me. Today is about the children.

I'm on time for my appointment. I locate Mr. Anderson's office easily. His secretary smiles pleasantly as I say, "Hi, I'm Emma Arnold. I'm here to see Mr. Anderson."

She responds politely, "He's expecting you. Please have a seat. I'll let him know you're here."

I sit and pick up a cooking magazine. Now here's another thing I'm not great at but wish I was. I love to eat and I love to eat good food. Instead of trying to make new things, I seem to make the same thing week after week.

I'm lost in the pictures of grilled chicken with various vegetables like zucchini and cauliflower. *Anyone can grill*, the magazine says. I respond by asking no one in particular, *Wanna bet?* when, suddenly, the secretary interrupts my thoughts, "Mr. Anderson will see you."

"Thank you," I say. I lay the magazine on the table and stand to walk into Mr. Anderson's office.

Mr. Anderson is a handsome man. He's over six feet tall and he has dark brown hair with a few streaks of grey. His brown eyes are warm and his smile stretches across his face in a charming manner. I even think his mustache is attractive, even though I'm not usually a fan.

"Hello, I'm Emma. I'm so grateful for your offer to help the children…" I start. I'm a little more nervous than I thought I was.

"It's my pleasure. Do you have a list of what you would like?" Mr. Anderson reaches for my paper. He nods as he scans the paper.

"I understand if you can't give everything…"

"Oh, yes. We can. This list is just what I was thinking you'd bring me when you told me there are seventeen children at the home and they range in ages from three to twelve." He's so sincere that I'm speechless for a moment.

My list includes hats of different styles and colors along with gloves for the older children and mittens for the younger children.

I also asked for each to have a new winter coat. In addition, boots are great at this time of year. For each girl, I ask for a dress with a slip and new underwear and stockings. For each boy, I ask for dress pants with a white shirt and tie. I know it seems like a lot, but Mr. Anderson instructed me to include everything I think the children would like.

"I can't tell you how grateful I am." I realize I keep saying grateful, but grateful is what I am. "These children are so dear to me. I have applied to adopt two of them...."

"That's wonderful," Mr. Anderson says, looking up from the list. "I admire you." His voice is so warm and kind.

"I wish I could take all of them home, to be honest."

Mr. Anderson smiles. "Let's see how we can help them have a *very* Merry Christmas!"

"Thank you again."

"My pleasure. I have your list, so let me get things together and I'll call you in a few days. How's that?"

"Sounds wonderful," I say and stand to leave. "Thanks again," I say as I stretch my hand out to shake his extended hand.

I leave and try not to be distracted by all the winter fashions I could spend all day looking at. I have more stops today.

As I drive to my next appointment at the toy store, I enjoy the Christmas music on the radio. *Jolly Old Saint Nicholas* is playing now. I sing along.

At the toy store, I'm meeting a lady named Ms. Westover. She sounds business-like on the phone, but when I arrive, I find her as warm and inviting as Mr. Anderson.

Ms. Westover is a short, round-built lady with grey

hair and spectacles she wears on a chain around her neck. She wears more makeup than many older women and bright red lipstick.

To be honest, I am fond of red lipstick. It reminds me of the pictures Grandpapa showed me of Grandmama. She always wore some eye shadow and very little blush, but he said she never left home without her red lipstick. I tried wearing red lipstick once, but thought I looked a little like a clown. *I'm going to try it again one day*, I think.

"How are you today, Miss Arnold?" Ms. Westover greets me cheerfully.

"I'm great. I can't tell you how much I appreciate your generosity to bless the children with toys for Christmas," I say.

"That's what the holiday season's all about, right?" Ms. Westover eases my anxiety with her kind words.

"Yes. These children are so precious. You should have seen them making their lists. They were very serious and took a great deal of time, making sure they included everything."

"I can imagine they did!" Ms. Westover chuckles as she agrees. She reminds me of the illustrations I've seen of Mrs. Claus in the books at the library. In my mind, I see her pulling a tray of fresh-baked cookies from an oven and offering them to everyone who enters her office.

"I understand if the lists are too long, but if they could just receive a thing or two on their lists..."

"Nonsense!" she snaps. "I looked over your lists, and they shall have everything we have to give them!"

I know that this is the final word! The children will have a BIG BIG Christmas. I can't help but smile. My heart is overwhelmed. I need to give her a hug. She sees me coming and accepts my gesture of thanks even though she's never met me before.

"I'll have all of Santa's elves gather these items, put them in boxes for you, and give you a call," Mrs. Westover tells me.

"I'm so grateful," I say. There's that word *grateful*

again. "I'll wait to hear from you. I can't thank you enough."

"Do you want us to wrap the gifts?" she offers.

"Oh, no. That's okay. I'll take care of that. I have help lined up." I say this with a smile, thinking of Evette and Jan's offer to help. We're going to have a wrapping party.

"Okay. We'll chat in a few days."

I leave and am overwhelmed with all the generosity I've experienced today. I'm definitely going to write Grandpapa to tell him about all this.

First, however, I stop at one of our favorite restaurants for a bowl of chicken noodle soup and a side of sourdough bread. Paw and I often stopped at this little 'mom and pop' restaurant that serves homemade food every day but Sunday. I try to sit in the same booth we sat in. The one by the front window. Paw and I would look out at the rain or snow or sunshine as we talked and ordered the same meal each time. Sitting here today makes me feel close to him.

After I finish my soup and bread, I arrive home and change clothes to my comfy sweats and a t-shirt with a bulky beige cardigan sweater. I sit at my kitchen counter with my cocoa with marshmallows and write my note to Grandpapa:

> *Dear Paw, Today I went to the stores that*
> *volunteered to donate the clothes and toys*
> *for the children. They are being SO generous*
> *I almost can't believe they are willing to give*
> *all the children a Christmas outfit they can*
> *wear to church service on Christmas Eve*
> *if they want as well as the toys they put on*
> *their Santa lists. I am grateful. Grateful is*
> *a word I've been using all day. I don't know*
> *another word to convey how I feel. It's just*
> *the same as I feel towards you and Charlie*
> *and Peter and Evette and Jan*
> *and Mrs. Carter and all the children…*
> *I better stop now. Will write more next time,*
> *Love, Emma.*

I put my coat on and walk to the cemetery. As I pass the park, I notice a young girl. It's odd to see just one person there, but she's the only one. I see her swinging, then she stops and walks to the picnic table and opens her backpack. She takes out a tablet and starts writing.

The park is a good place to write, especially if you're alone. It's a good place to think and put thoughts down on paper. It's easy to think and write in the park because it's quiet. Nature is soothing and always allows my thoughts to flow onto paper. I make up a story of what she's writing.

Maybe she's writing about a young girl walking in the woods and talking to all the animals. Or perhaps she's writing her inner feelings about chocolate cake and cookies. I'm being silly and think a few more plots to stories I'm sure she's not writing today.

I pass the park and continue on to see Paw. Today I see the groundskeeper. "Hello," I say. "I'm Emma. I visit my Grandpapa."

"Yes. I see you," he replies. "You leave the notes."

"I guess it's no secret."

"No. Everyone who comes here sees the mailbox. We think it's nice."

"Thank you. It seems someone has been leaving *me* notes in Paw's mailbox. Do you have any idea who it might be?"

"No. But I'm not here much. I only come to do light maintenance. I haven't seen anyone."

"Thanks anyway," I say. "I actually like the notes, I'm just not sure who leaves them."

"Someone you know, perhaps?"

"I would think so because they write as if they know me. In fact, they write as if they know me very well."

"*Friends* do things like that," he offers. I think it's nice of him to call whoever this is a 'friend.'

He's right. Would a stranger take time to do something so nice? I start to think of my friends and smile with each thought. Now, who would leave me notes? Probably all of them would. I'm not any closer to figuring out who it is.

"Thank you. I'm glad we've finally met. I have another note for my Grandpapa," I say. He nods as I walk away to put my note in the mailbox and have a little chat with Grandpapa.

15

Declined

I can't believe it's been an entire day without visiting Grandpapa. I've been so busy with the children and Christmas and finishing *Mother Gertie*, I didn't even retrieve my home mail for days. When I open my mailbox, the mail falls out all over the ground. Luckily, I manage to catch most of it and quickly snatch the rest from the ground. I stuff it all in my backpack and head to work.

When I arrive at work, Peter greets me with a huge grin on his face. I can see he's hiding something behind his back. "What do you have there, Peter?" I ask as I set my backpack on my desk.

"I have to tell you something," he starts to say.

"What is it?"

"Your little picture book…"

"*Mother Gertie*? What about it?"

"I put everything together-your pictures and story-and made a book!" Peter brings my little picture book from behind his back to show me.

"What …." I stammer. "But how?" I'm speechless.

"When you left the art and story on your desk, I scanned everything. Then, I put it all in a program to create the book and submitted it for printing….."

"I can't believe you did this," I interrupt him, partly happy, partly dazed.

"Emma, I know you only wrote it for yourself, but it's

really, really good," Peter says in a way begging me to forgive him for taking the pictures and story from my desk.

I stand at my desk flipping through the pages of my little book. I'm amazed at how beautiful it is.

"Well, I not only had the book made and printed, I also submitted it for an 'Excellence in Children's Literature' award. They will announce the winner in a few days."

"You did what?" I could barely get the words out of my mouth. "I can't believe it. You published my book *and* submitted it for an award?"

"Yes, Emma. The book is lovely and everyone thinks so. You should be proud. You're a talented author... and illustrator," he adds.

I sit at my desk and am quiet for a moment. I look at Peter long enough to make him uncomfortable.

"Are you mad?" he finally asks.

"No. I'm not mad, Peter. I just can't find the words to express how I feel. I can't find the words to thank you for doing this for me. This was *really* nice of you."

"I know," Peter says, smiling. "You're pretty nice yourself, you know."

"Thank you, Peter. I will treasure this forever."

"You could be famous, you know. Like Beatrix Potter and Dr. Seuss!" Peter seems to be more excited than I am.

"Not thinking that's going to happen," I say as I shake my head 'no.' The phone rings. I excuse myself to answer, "This is Emma." Peter goes back to restocking books.

I smile as my caller informs me that all my requests for clothing for the children have been granted. It was just yesterday afternoon that the toy store called me with the same great news. "I want to thank you so much. You are making such a great difference in these children's lives. They will be *so* happy this Christmas." I want to go on and on. I'm so thankful – and grateful.

I hang up and immediately call Charlie. My call goes to voicemail. "Charlie, it's Emma. Please call me when you get this."

I fumble through my mail as I wait for Charlie's call. "What's this?" I ask myself.

Suddenly, the phone rings. "This is Emma," I say as I begin opening an envelope from the Department of Family Services. My hands shake and I wonder what's inside? I tear the envelope opening it. Then I hear….

"Emma, it's Charlie." He sounds upset. His voice is strained and serious.

"What's wrong, Charlie?"

"Did you get the letter?"

"What letter?"

"About the adoption?"

"I think this is the letter. I'm opening the envelope now." I finish opening the envelope and unfold the letter. *"Thank you for your interest in adopting the children, but your application has been decl….."* I can't talk any longer.

"Emma?" I hear Charlie say. I can't talk. "Emma, I'm so sorry. I'll come right over."

"No. I want to be alone. I have to go." I hang up the phone.

Peter can see I'm not alright. "What's up, Em?" He's genuinely concerned.

"I have to go, Peter. Can you cover?"

"Sure." Peter picks up the letter I leave on the desk. I feel like I'm in a trance. I put my little book and thermos and lunch bag in my backpack. His smile over my little book turns into no expression at all as he watches me leave.

I can't go home, I tell myself. *I have to go to Paw.* I feel tears streaming down my face, but I can't remember starting to cry.

My heart is broken. I feel as if I've been hit in the stomach with a baseball bat. *Why? What do I do now?* The questions keep coming. *Am I just wishing for something that's impossible? How can I look at their room and not wish they were with me?* I keep walking. I don't even notice that it's very cold today and I didn't even close my coat. My boots slush through the snow as I make my way to Paw.

Snow is falling lightly. It seems appropriate that there's no one at the park today. All the tables are empty and there isn't anyone swinging on the swings or playing ball. In some strange way, this stillness and emptiness comfort me.

I feel desolate and defeated. I always knew they could say 'no' to me, but the truth is, I was never prepared for 'no.' I thought they would think I would be a wonderful mother and I would pass every test with flying colors. The twins would come home with me and we would be a family.

By the time I arrive at Paw's grave, I'm sobbing uncontrollably. I drop to my knees and put my face in my hands and cry until I cannot cry anymore.

I'm startled to feel a hand on my shoulder. I turn quickly to see Charlie standing there. "I'm here," is all he says.

I stand and turn into his arms. He holds me for what seems like hours. "How did you find me?" I ask.

"Where else would you be?" Charlie says gently, more as a statement of fact than a question.

"Why, Charlie? Why?"

"We're not sure. But Mrs. Carter and I are going to contact the Department of Family Services and ask. I don't want you to give up."

"Give up? They said 'no.' I read it. The exact word was DECLINED. Why?"

"The letter didn't say."

"How did you know?"

"We received a copy of the letter…"

"Of course. I should have known." I wipe my face and nose. "I was so expecting them to approve me. I thought the interviews and inspections all went well."

"I'm sure they did," Charlie says. "We want to ask them who made the decision and why they made this decision. We're going to get to the bottom of this, Emma. We can apply again."

"Thank you, Charlie. Thank Mrs. Carter, too."

"Emma, I have wanted to tell you for months how I feel about you…."

"What do you mean, Charlie?"

Charlie stands for a moment and then says, "If you think it would make a difference, I'm willing to marry you."

"Charlie. I do love you, but I can't marry you just to adopt the girls." I stand speechless for a moment. I have never said this out loud before and here I'm blurting it out so easily. I never admitted I *love* him before.

"It's not just the girls. I *want* to marry you. I didn't think they would decline the adoption. But you know I love those twins too, and I do love you. I finally said it."

"It means everything to me to hear you offer this, Charlie, but I really need to know that when I marry, I marry someone for the right reason and not just to convince Family Services I would make a suitable mother to adopt the twins. And…." I catch myself rambling. "I want to know someone's marrying me for the right reasons…"

"You'll be a great mother," Charlie interrupts and then insists, "But I do want to marry you for the right reasons as well as I want you to have everything you want."

"We have to talk about this later. I'm so exhausted. I am so disappointed. I left work and Peter's covering for me."

"I know. He called to let me know."

"Did you know he made my story into a real book and submitted it for an award?" Somehow, this happy event in my life is not enough to take away the pain in my heart. I show him the book.

"Yes. He told me that, too. It's wonderful." As Charlie flips through my book, he says, "It's a reflection of you and how beautiful you are, Emma."

"Thank you, but how does everyone know everything before I do?" I don't really want an answer.

Charlie and Peter are friends and I love them both *like* friends, but now I love Charlie in a different and romantic way. His proposal has made this clear to me, even though I can't accept it.

"Let me drive you home," Charlie offers.

At first, I really want to stay close to Grandpapa. Then

I realize I'm freezing. The weather has chilled even more since I came to see Grandpapa, and the wind has picked up.

When we arrive at my home, Charlie walks inside with me and thoughtfully helps me sort my belongings. He unpacks my papers and *Mother Gertie* book from my backpack and places everything on the table. "Can I make you some cocoa or tea?" he asks.

"Some green tea with tupelo honey would be great if you don't mind."

"I don't mind." Charlie reaches into the cupboard for a mug. Then he spots the tea on the counter next to the honey. He moves around my kitchen as if he's been here before. I don't ever remember him being in my home.

I take a deep breath and feel slightly warmer, so I take my coat off and relax at the kitchen counter.

"I'm going to give you my home number and my cell number," Charlie says.

"I'll be alright."

"I know. But if you need to talk. I want you to call me immediately. It doesn't matter what time it is."

I know he means this. He takes a pen from my pen jar on the counter and, as he writes his name and home phone and cell phone numbers, I'm stunned. I see the writing. This is the handwriting on my letters in Grandpapa's mailbox.

"You sent me the letters?"

Charlie stops writing and stands still. He doesn't move and he doesn't talk. I don't move. I don't talk.

We stare at each other for what seems like light-years. Charlie's apparently waiting to see what my true reaction to this revelation will be.

I think lots of thoughts. I wonder how he knows that I play piano and violin and dance and write and had a date and love gardening. *How does he know me so well?* I ask myself.

I don't want to be angry. My letters are private and my thoughts are private, but this doesn't matter right now. The letters have meant so much to me. They have touched my heart in a way nothing has since I lost my Grandpapa.

Deep down, I'm glad it's been Charlie sending me the notes. I'm glad he feels the same about me that I do about him. We've never even had a date. But it seems we've had so many dates. Every time I see the children, I see Charlie. We share time together. We share moments of giving to and loving the children.

Finally, I get up. Charlie watches me go to the windowsill and fetch a small tin box labeled, 'TREASURES.' I bring the box to the counter and open it. I take out the notes.

More tears. "I can't tell you how much these little notes have meant to me, Charlie. I had no idea you sent them." I pick up what I call my 'music' note. "When you wrote and encouraged me to play the piano, I couldn't figure out who knew I played and how I played. Then I decide it doesn't really matter. I take so much pleasure playing and was so happy to be encouraged this way."

Then I took out the note about my art. "How do you know I'm an artist?"

"You doodle when you come to the orphanage. Sometimes you leave your sketch pad on the table."

"Oh. I see. I don't even realize I do this. You pay attention, Mr. Charlie," I say, mimicking the children. "I do love art. Your note is the reason I did Gertie's illustrations."

"Yes."

I open the letters about loving dance and wishing I was a *real* writer. "I love these notes. I do love to dance and I love my little Gertie book. Thank you." Charlie nods as I hug my *Mother Gertie* book.

"Now I realize why you never asked about my pizza thing with Peter," I say as I unfold the note that I will 'know when the right person comes along.'

Charlie doesn't say anything.

"I love my little note about gardening even when the flowers don't come up. I will plant them anyway. I guess you read my notes about Thanksgiving and sledding and getting all the donations for the children…"

Charlie nods.

I stop for a moment and then take out the last note. "But I cried from the deepest parts of my being when I read this little note. It means the most to me." I read his note about my adopting the girls :

To my beautiful Emma, don't let the fear of failure stop you. Run after and catch all your dreams. You will make a wonderful mother. You have so much love in your heart to give those twins and they will be forever grateful for you. You will have no regrets. I have no regrets taking you home to love and share your life with. You will have them to share their life with and they will have you to share their lives with. Love works both ways. You rescue each other. You will be a GREAT mom.

I'm sure I see a small tear trickle from Charlie's eyes. He hugs me again. "I do love you, Emma."

"I love you too, Charlie. I have never known anyone but Grandpapa and you, who know me so well and love me so much."

I wipe my face and chuckle as I admit this to him.

"Can I do anything else for you?" he asks.

"Not right now. I've had a *BIG* day. A book published, being rejected for adopting my beautiful Sarah and Susan, discovering you're the letter bandit and letter writer, and being proposed to. Now it all makes sense. Now the letters all make sense."

Charlie smiles. "I'm so happy to know you, Emma. We're going to get to the bottom of this and everything will work out..."

I adore it when he says, 'we' all the time. He really is in my corner.

"My offer still stands."

"I will keep that in mind. I need to rest."

"I understand. You have my number." Charlie kisses me on my left cheek.

As he goes to the door, I remember my phone call at the library. "Charlie."

"Yes, Emma."

"I forgot to tell you. The clothing company is going to donate coats, hats, gloves, boots, a pair of shoes, and a new outfit for every child at the orphanage."

"You know we get donations."

"I know. But I wanted the children to have something *new,* all for themselves."

"That's wonderful. How did you manage…."

"That's not important. I think many people are very generous. They are willing."

"Ok," Charlie says.

"Also, I took the Santa lists and the toy store is going to donate almost all the items on the lists."

"That's amazing, Emma. How?"

"Again, not important. I want the children to have a wonderful Christmas and I think they will all get what's on their lists. I can purchase whatever they don't donate. Tony asked for a ride on a real train. I'm still working on that."

"You are amazing. I can't wait to see what you come up with next."

After Charlie leaves, I slip onto my bed and quietly sob until I fall asleep.

myflowerjournal.com

16

Power Ride

I wake slowly today - still feeling the sadness of rejection and not sure I really want to get out of bed. I stew about life and what to do next. I'm so confused. As I lie in bed, my thoughts drift to everything that has happened over the past few months.

I tell myself I can't lie here forever, so I slip out of bed and head to the kitchen. I pass the girls' bedroom, but don't look in. I know I'll start crying again.

I will not give in to self-pity and remind myself that Charlie and Mrs. Carter will help sort things out so I can reapply to adopt Sarah and Susan.

It's time to get going this morning. A power ride on my bicycle is just what I need to get myself out of this funk! Some challenging exercise and the cool air in my face will surely help my doldrums.

I put the kettle on to make a quick cup of tea with tupelo honey. Then, I return to my bedroom to dress for my ride on this cool, early winter day in Ohio. I don't mind a cooler ride. I find it invigorating.

It's actually a perfect morning for a bike ride, with very little wind and temperatures hovering around fifty-five degrees. The recent snows we had melted in the warmer temperatures, and the really heavy snows and frigidly cold weather don't usually come until after Christmas, but one never knows what's in store in Ohio.

I pull on my form-fitting spandex riding pants along with bulky white socks and my lamb's wool insulated boots. I decide on a turtleneck with a navy sweatshirt and a zip-up heavy sweater. I wrap a knit scarf around my neck in case I need to cover my face and mouth. The final touch is my pink knit headband that covers my forehead and ears.

My bike is an older model JAMIS racing bike. It's as light as a feather and is the fastest bike I've ever ridden. I start out my drive and shift into seventh gear as I head to the bike path that circles along the edge of town. I'm alone on the path and think to myself *It's too cold for most people, but not me!*

My legs burn for a few minutes as I pump harder and harder, picking up speed and, in the next moment, it feels as if the bike and I have become one as we sail through the air.

One of the things I like most about my bike is that no matter how fast I'm going, whenever I pedal, the chain is always engaged and there is no slipping feeling I used to feel on other bikes when the bike was going faster than my peddle mechanism.

While I ride this quiet morning, my thoughts drift to when I was a young girl and those early days of living with my *most wonderful and dearest Grandpapa* after I lost my parents in that awful car accident.

Grandpapa made me feel secure and safe from the moment I carried my small suitcase through the front door. I was too young to realize how deeply he, too, must have felt the loss of my mother, his daughter, and how lonely he must have already been after Grandmama passed. I only saw life as it pertained to me. Now that I'm an adult, I have empathy for what others may be experiencing. Looking back, we were good company for each other. We needed each other.

Grandpapa always stopped whatever he was doing when I got home from school, and we'd have a snack together while I did my homework at the kitchen table. Some days, he'd take me to his workshop behind the house and let me help with his latest project. It could have been repairing a rocking chair runner or making the cutest little birdhouses.

We would hang the birdhouses close to the house or in the yard and watch the birds coming and going. He could sit and listen to them sing for hours and never complained about the mess they left on the side porch. I learned to clean up the mess at a very young age. Squirrels also came for a snack.

Grandpapa wasn't the best cook in the world but, thankfully, I've never been a picky eater. I eat whatever someone has cared enough to make for me. His best meal was roast beef with carrots. Sometimes it was a little dry, but it went down much easier with jarred gravy and the lumpy mashed potatoes I helped make.

By age ten, I had learned how to make simple things like tasty tuna-noodle casserole and scrambled eggs. Luckily, Grandpapa wasn't a picky eater either. Once, after we had tuna casserole, I overheard him say to one of my aunts, 'It didn't *look* so good, but it *tasted* just fine.' I smiled. He didn't know I heard him.

When neither of us felt up to cooking, we'd get our favorite fast food - burgers and fries. We became French fry connoisseurs and tried every place in town to uncover the mystery of where the *very* best fries were. Hands down, it was Ma's Diner that made our favorite and best fries. They were crispy with just the right amount of salt.

But the truth is that many times we were rescued by Paw's wonderful lady friend who lived across the street. She made sure we always had something good. If we didn't cook, she did. Everyone needs a neighbor like Rita.

Paw knew I wanted to be a librarian and, in my senior year of high school, he encouraged me to apply for grants so I could attend a local college where I studied English and History.

Looking back, I think he liked the idea of my staying at home instead of going off to college. We continued having our afternoon snacks while I did my college homework too. He cheered me on and continued to take me on our French fry expeditions all the way to my Master's degree in Library Science.

The best day of my life was when Paw told me how proud he was of me. He told me it took courage to do what I did. Grandpapa valued education. I suppose it was because he knew the value of an education. He only had an eighth-grade education because he had to drop out of school to work to help care for his family. Nevertheless, he is the smartest man I have ever known.

It was only six months after I finished college that I lost Grandpapa. Saddest day of my life. It was even worse than losing my parents because I had most of my memories with him. I hope he knows how much he has meant to me and still does. It is because of his love and tender care that I have accomplished all the things I have.

Paw always urged me to try everything that caught my interest. He's the one who took me to the church to play the piano and to dance sessions. He even took me horseback riding on a rare occasion.

He gave me the home I still live in and have never had a desire to leave. Why would I? The happiest days of my life have been spent here.

The house is forever filled with love and laughter and joy. And, on days like this, when I'm at my lowest, the memories surround me and lift me out of my sorrow. The mailbox keeps us in touch.

When I started visiting the orphanage, I felt at home there too. It's strange how a place and everyone there can feel so comfortable the minute you walk in the door.

I interrupt my thoughts to look at my watch. Ten minutes have passed - which means I've ridden about two miles. I stop on the side of the path, just missing a squirrel racing across the path.

I'm so deep in thought that I don't notice my hands are cold. I'm glad I remembered my gloves. I reach into my pockets and pull out my favorite pair of red knit gloves. I put them on my half-frozen hands and continue my power ride.

I'm happy to see a cardinal this morning. As I mentioned before, they not only remind me of my father, now they remind me of Paw too. I can watch them flutter from tree branch to tree branch without realizing how much time passes. They will always be my fave. On with my ride!

Where was I? Oh, yeah. The orphanage. I remember the day I met Charlie. I walked through the main entrance and noticed an open door to an office on the right. I poked my head in and there sat Charlie. *What a handsome man*, I thought. He had the warmest smile and a formidable handshake. As he leaned over his desk and stretched his hand my way, my arm and hand involuntarily moved in his direction.

"I'm Emma,"

"I'm Charlie," he replied. "What can we do for you?"

I stood in front of his desk without knowing exactly what to say. "I'm Emma," I said again, embarrassed.

He graciously smiled and asked, "Is there something you'd like us to do for you?"

"Oh, I'm sorry," I started. "I'm a little nervous."

"Don't be nervous. You're among friends."

I continued, "I was wondering if I could help with the children." I was relieved to remember what I came for.

"Help?" he asked quizzically.

"What I mean is, I mean, I love children. I'm a children's librarian. The head librarian, to be specific. I wonder if I could come and lead story time and do a small craft or activity with the children? Or something?" I stammer and talk quickly. If he wasn't so darn nice and cute. Did I mention he's handsome? "I have so many ideas and am used to teaching children…. what I mean is I have taught children and have story time at the library all the time, and want to share my time and read to the children here and…."

"I think that can be arranged." He rescued me from my rambling thoughts and words the moment I met him.

"Thank you," I said softly, finally calmer.

"I'll take a look at our activities calendar and we can arrange a time that's convenient for you to come."

We exchanged contact information and he called two days later with a date to get started. I was so glad he wasn't just being kind, he warmly invited me to the orphanage.

The first day I arrived at the orphanage, I brought a picture book about caterpillars becoming butterflies. I also filled a huge sack with art and craft supplies to make little thumbprint paintings of cute butterflies on small canvases. I brought child-safe red, blue, orange, yellow, and green finger paint, the two-inch canvases, and small wooden easels to hold the canvas art. Like the ones Peter and I used at the library.

As Charlie directed me to the activity room, he said, "We've been looking forward to your visit."

I was nervous about how the children would receive me, but five seconds with Charlie made me feel welcome and as if I could do anything. He stayed to help.

Suddenly, my thoughts are interrupted as I hear, "HEADS UP!" I look up in time to swerve quickly, avoiding an oncoming bicyclist. I'm surprised to see someone else on the path! As we pass each other, we nod, and I call out, "I'm so sorry. Didn't think anyone else was riding this cool morning."

"No problem….." I hear his words drifting into the cool air behind me as he whizzes by.

After this near miss, I decide I'd better pay more attention. I come to a slight hill and kick my bike into a slightly easier gear to negotiate the uphill ride.

I struggle for what seems an eternity, but is probably just about three minutes. Then, ZOOM! I fly down the other side of the hill at top speed with the wind blowing my ponytails behind me. Thank goodness for the warmth of my knit headband. I need the warmth of my scarf, so, at the bottom of the hill, I stop to pull it over my nose and mouth.

I concentrate on my ride for a few more miles and, when I check the time, I'm surprised to see I've been riding for twenty minutes and still feel like I just started my ride. This makes me feel good to know I'm stronger than when I first started riding several years ago. I used to tire quickly and needed frequent breaks. Now, I make it to my destination five miles from home and all the way back without getting winded or needing a break.

My mind continues to drift. The letters are my way of feeling connected to Grandpapa, and now I feel connected to Charlie too. I never suspected he was the one writing back to me. And asking me to marry him. Where did that come from? That was a sweet thing to do, but I have so many mixed emotions about it. There are moments when I wish I had said, 'Yes.' I picture the four of us in my happy little cottage home, doing homework around the kitchen table as Grandpapa and I used to do. Gee, I hope Charlie is a better cook.

Will it be difficult to see him since I said, 'No?' I'm sure he won't make me feel awkward about it, but what is *he* feeling? Did he ask me just to help me adopt the girls? Or does he have genuine feelings for me? Is he confusing compassion with love? No. He was definitely sincere.

But marriage *is* about so much more than just liking someone or raising children. It's a lifelong commitment that would last long after the girls leave home to start lives of their own. We need to have something in common other than parenthood. And I need to feel that he loves me for me, even if the girls aren't part of the equation.

As I round the next bend in the path, I encounter another distraction; an elderly man walking his tan, short-haired Chihuahua dressed in a perfectly fitted argyle sweater. He's walking nicely on his leash. They don't see me right away, so I slow to avoid hitting them since they're wandering from side to side along the paved path.

I chuckle as he startles and says, "I'm so sorry, I didn't see you or hear you coming."

"That's alright. I needed a short break," I say with light-hearted laughter in my voice. I pull my bike over to stop next to him.

"Cool morning for a ride, isn't it?"

"Yes, but I welcome the coolness. I really enjoy the park at this time of year, and my bike gets me here and home quickly."

"That looks like a nice bike," he remarks.

"It's a racing bike, but I don't race. I just like that it's light and fast. It has a number of gears that can make it an easy ride or, like today, a more challenging ride. I thought I'd stay warmer if I worked a little harder."

"I think that's wise," he says with a smile.

"Pretty cool for you and your pup, too, eh? I see you two are all bundled up," I comment.

"I walk on the path early in the morning. Chico and I walk every day; even when it snows, which will probably be soon. I sense these things."

"Sooner than I like," I say.

"Ohio."

"Yes. I know. I'd better get moving. I'm getting a little chilled. It's nice to meet you. I'm Emma," I say as I offer my hand.

"I'm Roger," he replies and gives me a firm shake. "Stay warm and get home safely."

"You too," I say as I get moving along on the bike.

I check my watch again and see I've been riding for thirty-five minutes. That's a little longer than I wanted to do in my outbound direction, but I've been so lost in my thoughts, I don't realize how far I've been riding.

I slowly turn my bike around and head for home. I keep the gears the same and make it home as a light snow begins falling. "Yep. It's winter in Ohio."

17

The Award and Accepted

Getting the house ready for the girls reminds me of the benefits of a healthier breakfast. I might have used the yogurt and applesauce to show Ms. O'Brien that I would provide good choices for the girls, but children copy what they see. I could be a better role model for healthy eating, and I vow I will be.

So, I make myself a nutritious breakfast before I head into work today. I fry eggs over easy, drop two slices of whole-grain bread into the toaster, pour some orange juice, and add a banana to my plate.

Since I'm feeling stuffed after my bigger-than-usual breakfast, a visit to the cemetery to drop off another letter will be just the thing I need to walk off the heavy meal.

It's sad to think that now that the cat is out of the bag, and Charlie has confessed he's the one writing the letters, that I won't be receiving any more of them, but it's ok. My letter today says,

> *Dear Paw, I haven't been told why*
> *I was turned down for the adoption*
> *and I'm afraid to ask. I can change*
> *anything about the house they ask me*
> *to, but what if it's me they don't like? I*
> *can't change myself. Charlie and*
> *Mrs. Carter said they will help me sort*
> *this out, but I'm struggling to keep a*

I spend a few more moments with Paw and then it's on to the library. When I arrive at the library, I see there are more cars than usual in the parking lot, and the van from the orphanage is parked near the front door. *What's going on?* I wonder.

I open the door and see Charlie with Sarah and Susan standing in the hallway. "Well, this is a happy surprise. What's going on?" I ask.

"Hi, Miss Emma!" Susan exclaims.

"Congradiations," Sarah adds.

"Hello, my precious girls!!" I exclaim right back as they leap into my arms. I can barely pick both of them up at one time. Charlie comes to my rescue, taking Susan into his arms. "What's going on?" I ask him again.

"You'll see," is all he says.

The library is overflowing with the children from the orphanage plus many faces I recognize as library regulars from the neighborhood. Peter is standing at my desk, dressed in a goose suit, surrounded by chattering, bouncy children. "Good morning, Peter. What's going on? And why are you dressed like that?" I ask, definitely impressed.

"We're celebrating," Peter says as if it's obvious.

"And what are we celebrating?"

"You," Peter answers matter-of-factly.

"Me? And why are we celebrating me?"

"You won the award for your *Mother Gertie* book."

"How....When.. Who??" Peter hands a copy of my book with a shiny little sticker on the cover that reads 'Excellence in Children's Literature - First Place.'

He steps aside to reveal a poster with a photo of me and a picture of my book. I'm speechless. Charlie's smiling, the kids are talking to me, but I can only stare at my book.

"I told you I submitted it. You won," Peter says as if

it's the most natural thing in the world.

"I'm stunned. I never expected this. WOW!" is all I can say. "Your goose suit is adorable," I say to Peter with a warm smile.

"Can we sit with you at your desk?" Sarah asks.

"Yeah. Can we?" Susan chimes in. "We want to be libraries too."

"Of course," I say and pull out my chair. Sarah and Susan both squeeze onto the chair. They pretend they are librarians and straighten the papers on the desk and ring the bell I placed there for children or parents to get my attention when I'm elsewhere in the library. They take pens and pencils from my terracotta pencil holder.

Peter allowed the children to run rampant in the children's section of the library before I arrived. Now he struggles to calm the bedlam. "Children," he says. "Let's all gather on the story carpet for Emma to read her book!" He sounds more excited than I do for this award. "Miss Emma won an award because her book is so special. Let's all shout and tell her 'CONGRATULATIONS."

"Congratulations," they all say at once. Some say "Congradiates."

"Thank you, children. I'm so glad you're all here today. You all look so wonderful. How about we read about Goose Gertie?"

"Yes," they say as they all find a place on the carpet. Susan and Sarah stay at my desk. It's fun pretending to be the librarian.

I sit on the story time stool and, as I hold my book, I look at Peter in his goose suit and ask, "Would *you* like to read today, Peter?"

"I think the honor is all yours, Emma," he says kindly.

"Well, I wouldn't have won the award if it weren't for you. Plus, I'm overwhelmed," I say softly.

"If you put it that way, sure." Peter takes the book from me and begins reading while I sit with the twins. Charlie pulls a chair close to my desk as well. The assistants from the orphanage keep an eye on the other children who are behaving extremely well today.

After reading the book, Peter looks up and asks, "And who likes *Mother Gertie : A Mother Goose*?"

"I do. I do," they all say.

"Then we must all enjoy some cake and ice cream!" Peter exclaims.

Peter decorated tables in the activity area with tablecloths with 'Congratulations' printed on them, along with matching plates and napkins. He somehow managed to find a baker to make cakes in the shape of a goose! *How cute is all this?* I think. *He thought of everything.*

As Charlie, the assistants, and a few parents serve the children their drinks, cake, and ice cream, I sit at my desk flipping through the pages of my book. This makes me happy even with all the unhappiness I'm feeling at the same time. There's no word from Mrs. Carter or Charlie about the reasons the adoption was declined, and I'm afraid to ask.

Charlie brings Sarah and Susan their cake and ice cream, and then returns with servings for himself and me.

"Thank you, Charlie," I say. "I'm so happy you and the children came today. How did you manage.….?"

"You know I can I do anything!" He winks.

"Yes. I know. And you do." I smile. "I'm always wondering how you'll surprise me next."

"Hang on and you'll find out," Charlie says with a big smile on his face.

How can he be so happy when I'm so crushed? Although, it's nice to be distracted for a moment with this surprise celebration. Who would have thought I would be an award-winning author? I rub my fingers over the medal on the cover and it makes it more real.

Thankfully, no one mentions, or perhaps they haven't noticed, how much I'm like Mother Gertie. I want to be a mother too. I want the girls to tell me what they want for breakfast, lunch, and dinner, and what they want to watch on television. I imagine a nightly routine of reading books, bath time, tucking them into their beds, and turning off their lights….

It's easy to get lost in my thoughts as I watch the girls eating their cake and ice cream and laughing and talking without a care in the world. They are perfect librarians. They don't even know I have a bedroom waiting for them…

"Emma."

I'm startled to hear Mrs. Carter's voice as she taps my shoulder. "I didn't expect to see you today…" I say.

"Hello, Mizzizz Carter," the twins say together. "We're the libraries today. Can we help you get a book?"

"Good to see you, children. I don't want a book right now, but I'll let you know in a few minutes." Mrs. Carter touches their faces and then turns her attention to me, "I wanted to talk to you in person, Emma. Is there somewhere we can talk?"

"Sure. Girls, I need to chat with Mrs. Carter. How about you stay here and be the librarians?" I say as I lift Sarah from my lap and place her next to Susan on my overly large chair.

"Is something wrong?" I ask Mrs. Carter. I'm nervous now. Seeing her has made my heart skips a few beats.

"Charlie, can you join us, please?" Mrs. Carter sounds so business-like.

"I can," Charlie says as he puts Tony down in a chair next to my desk. "Hey, champ, you sit while I talk. I'll be right back."

"Ok," Tony says as he turns his attention quickly to the other children.

I show Mrs. Carter and Charlie to a conference room. "We can chat privately here," I say, waving them in.

"Thank you," Mrs. Carter says. Charlie follows her and they both take a seat.

"I'll get to the point quickly. I know my being here is a surprise to you, Emma," Mrs. Carter smiles to reassure me.

"Well, actually it is," is all I can manage to say.

"Charlie and I requested that the board provide the

reasons they declined your adoption application for Sarah and Susan."

She hesitated for a moment. It seemed like the longest hesitation of my life. I didn't move or say a word, but thoughts filled my mind. *I imagine a hundred scenarios. They don't think my job is stable. They think my house is too small. They don't think I know enough about children. I'm too young, not young enough? What could it be??*

"It's good news," Charlie says, because he sees tears welling up in my eyes.

Thoughts continue swirling in my head. *How can it be good news? They've turned me down. Are they expecting me to change something about myself? Buy a bigger house? Learn how to cook better?*

"When the adoption agency checked their files, they realized they had made a clerical mistake, Emma. You *have been* granted the adoption." Mrs. Carter jumps in.

More tears. This time for joy. I'm overwhelmed. "I don't understand?" I manage to say.

"They mixed up your file with another client's. The other client didn't submit all their paperwork, which is why they were declined. By mistake, the agency put *their* papers in *your* file. When the secretary opened the file, she didn't notice the other client's name on the paperwork; she just saw yours on the folder. She wrote the letter informing you that you were declined, but the letter was meant for the other client."

She hesitates again to allow this to sink in. Charlie takes my hand and gives it a gentle squeeze.

"Everyone who reviewed your references, your interviews, and your inspection reports agrees you're a perfect candidate to adopt Sarah and Susan," Mrs. Carter says as she hands me the acceptance letter.

I take the paper and read as well as I can as tears flow down my cheeks. "I can't thank you and Charlie enough, Mrs. Carter. I'm so happy. I can't believe they're going to be mine. What happens next?"

"Well, it probably won't be finalized until after the

holidays, but the ball is rolling and it's just a matter of time."

"I know Sarah and Susan will be happy too," Charlie says, standing over me, reading my acceptance letter. *Is that a small tear I see in the corner of his eye?*

I mouth the words, *thank you,* as I turn and look into his beautiful, kind eyes.

The three of us return to the party to see that Sarah and Susan have written their names on a paper to identify themselves as the new librarians. "Are you girls helping everyone find books?" Mrs. Carter asks.

"We are," Susan responds with complete confidence.

"They are cute," I say to Charlie.

"Yes," he agrees. "So how are your holiday plans coming along?" Charlie asks.

"I visited the stores donating the children's gifts and have been promised the things on our lists and the children's Santa lists. I have to pick up everything tomorrow. Evette and Jan are coming over in the evening to wrap presents and eat pizza."

"Do you need any more help?"

"You're kind to offer, but we're making a girls' night out of it. But I will need help getting everything to the orphanage."

"I'm happy to help. Just let me know when."

Charlie gathers up the children - including my librarians - and heads to the van. "See you tomorrow?"

"Yes," I say. "Thank you for everything."

"My pleasure. Congratulations - on both the book and being a mom." He smiles.

When they leave, I sit at my desk and look over the room. The other children have left as well. It's quiet once again.

It's been a great day. Who would have ever thought I would be an award-winning children's author? And accepted for an adoption I dreamt about. And, I have a special man in my life. At this moment, I know I'm going to tell him 'Yes.'

18

Toys, Clothes, and Engaged

Tomorrow is Christmas Eve. Planning to spend Christmas Eve and Christmas Day with the children and Charlie has given me so much more to do than my usual holidays alone. Charlie's spending lots of time with the children. Seems Charlie's pretty much an orphan too.

The library's closing early today, so everyone can have more time to enjoy the holidays, will help me get all my errands done. I have a long list.

First, I have to pick up the presents and clothes, get them sorted, and wrap the presents. Then, I need to get the clothes to the orphanage so the children can wear their new things to the Christmas Eve service. Charlie said he'd help take the clothes over today and help take presents over after the children are in bed tomorrow, so they can find them when they wake up on Christmas morning. Thank goodness I don't have to do any cooking or baking.

As I sit making my 'to-do' list, Peter walks over and asks, "Hey, Emma. How are you?"

"Good. Lots to do this holiday. How about you? What are your plans?"

"I have Christmas Eve dinner with my mom every year and then, on Christmas Day, I go to a homeless shelter in town and have dinner with them. My church puts together little gift boxes filled with personal items and snacks so they have something for Christmas."

I stop making my list and look up at Peter with a surprised look on my face. "I didn't know that. How precious. I'll bet they really enjoy your company. What do you have for dinner?"

"Dinner with Mom is small. She fixes a turkey breast, mashed potatoes, and some vegetables. We open our presents and spend the whole evening together. At the homeless shelter, the meal is much bigger! We have all the regular things; turkey, stuffing, yams, and cranberry sauce. We also have homemade apple and pumpkin pies. Local chefs come and prepare the meal and we all give thanks and eat together. I take some small gifts I think they'd like in addition to the boxes my church donates. We drink eggnog and talk like we've never left the year before. We also sing carols and enjoy dessert; we usually have ice cream or whipped cream on the apple and pumpkin pie!"

"Sounds quite charming. I love it. You really are a great guy, Peter. It's very generous of you to share your time."

"Well, thanks. I enjoy spending time with them. There are so many people who are alone on the holidays, and I have so much to be thankful for."

"We all do, really. Peter, I want to thank you again for your support and for taking the time to put *Mother Gertie* together *and* having it published *and* entering it into the Excellence in Children's Literature contest, *and* having the award party. You really went above and beyond the call of friendship."

"It was my pleasure, Emma. The story is cute. You did a good job. It's a beautiful message. It made me want to have children too," Peter says with a small smile.

"I'm glad. Anyway, it was just an idea I put on paper and drew some pictures for, but you made this happen." I look at Peter with the most gratitude I can muster. He nods.

"Glad we're only working half a day today," Peter says. "We can both use the extra time to do our *good deeds*!"

"That's for sure!" I agree.

After our short day, I pack up everything and head to see Grandpapa. I found a small decorated Christmas wreath to place on his grave. I drive today because it's so cold, and I have to retrieve the clothes and presents after my visit.

I have a short letter to leave Grandpapa about Christmas and how I remember all our Christmases together. I write that I'm not rejected, I'M ACCEPTED! and the girls will be mine. I also tell him I'm going to say, 'Yes' to Charlie. He'll understand.

There are more people than usual in the cemetery today. I realize it's because it's Christmas. I know holidays are the most difficult days for those who have lost loved ones. They are missed more on the holidays, even though they're missed every day. No one stops missing the ones they love.

The wind is quite cold today, so I don't want to stay too long. When I open the mailbox, I'm surprised to see a letter and a small box. "Oh, Charlie. What do we have here?"

As I read the note, tears stream down my face. Tears seem to be flowing more and more these days. The little box is from a jewelry store. I can only imagine what's inside. I'll wait to open it until I get to the orphanage. I drop my letter in the mailbox and blow a kiss to Grandpapa. "Merry Christmas, Paw." In the distance, I hear church bells ringing.

I'd better get going. Lots to do before Evette and Jan come over. I make my way to the toy store first. If I have to, I can lay clothes over the toys if I'm crunched for space.

And crunched I am. I cannot believe the number of toys the staff loads into my car. Boxes of stuffed animals, a train set for Paulie, that fire truck Tony wants, and the dolls! There are so many dolls and Barbie accessories.

"I'm not sure my car is big enough," I say, worried.

"We'll get it to fit, don't you worry about that!" The staff is excited to help me. Christmas really is the season for giving.

"I can't believe this," I say to Ms. Westover. More tears.

"It's our pleasure. We want you to give those children our best!" she exclaims. "And I wanted to give *you* this."

Ms. Westover hands me a small box. I open it and smile as I see a tube of red lipstick. "Oh, my," I say as I take the gift.

"I noticed you staring at mine. Your light pink is quite nice, but try the red. It really does something for you."

"I will. This is so kind of you. I will wear it with joy," I say. We hug.

"We can't fit anymore in the front or back seat. Do you have any room in your trunk?" one of the staff members asks.

"I do." I open my trunk and we fit the remaining toys there.

"Thank you again and again and again," I say as I hug each one of them and Ms. Westover one more time. As I hug her, I whisper, "I'm going to adopt two of the children."

"That's wonderful, Dear," she says with a smile.

I cry happy tears all the way to the clothing store. They're going to think I'm some crazy woman crying and driving around with a car filled with toys.

When I walk into the clothing store, I see Mr. Anderson helping with last-minute sales in the men's section.

"Good afternoon, Mr. Anderson," I say.

"Emma. We have all your items. Do you want the hangers with the clothes?"

"Maybe. But I have a small car, so I need to make sure they fit over the toys the toy store donated for the children."

"That's wonderful. Let me call Troy over to help load the clothes."

It's a tight squeeze, but we manage to get all the clothes into my car without wrinkling them – shoes, boots, hats, and all!

I'm off to home and, to my surprise, Charlie's waiting for me. "Hi. Have you been waiting long?" I ask.

"Nope. I just got here. I stopped by the library and saw it's closed. Thought I might find you here." He stoops to look in my car. "Looks like a huge heist," he says with a giggle.

I ignore his insinuation that I heisted the clothes and toys. "I just picked up the clothes and toys. You're not going to believe how many toys they donated."

"I'll help get them inside," Charlie offers.

We unload the clothes and set them across the girls' beds and place the shoes and boots on the floor.

"This is a really nice room you made for the girls," he says as he looks at everything and reads the poems on the name plaques over their beds. "The girls will love this."

"Thank you. I did all this before the agency declined my adoption. Then it was difficult to see the room….."

"I'm glad everything worked out."

"Me too. Thank you for all you did for me."

"Oh, before I forget, I got the girls something too. I'm going to give these to them for Christmas, but thought I'd bring them today to show you…" Charlie says as he pulls two small boxes from his pocket.

I open the boxes with small gold heart-shaped necklaces inside with the letter 'S' on each of them. "Charlie, these are darling," I say as I make much over them.

"I'm glad you like them. I got all the girls the same and picked out wallets for the boys with their names on them."

Charlie isn't as talkative as he usually is, and he's quite fidgety today. It dawns on me that he may want to know if I was at the cemetery this morning.

"The toys are going to be a real challenge to unload."

"We'll get 'em," Charlie says with confidence.

I'm glad he came. There really are a lot of toys. "I even have some in the trunk. I received all the gifts that were on the children's lists. Evette and Jan will be here in a couple of hours to help wrap and put name tags on each gift," I say as we stack the last of the toys in my living room. I can barely move around, but I manage to get to the kitchen with Charlie right behind me. "Would you like some cocoa or tea?" I ask.

"Hot cocoa would be nice, thank you."

As I begin making the cocoa for each of us, I know I can't torture him any longer and say, "I visited my Grandpapa today…"

"Really?" he perks up.

"Yes. I found a note and a small box inside his mailbox."

"You did?"

"Yes. I did. I think you know about it."

I finish fixing the hot cocoa and add a dollop of whipping cream to each of our cups. Charlie waits patiently for me to continue. I sip a little cocoa before I do.

"I brought the box home with me, but haven't opened it yet. Should I open it now?"

"Okay," is all Charlie says.

I fetch my coat and put my hand into the side pocket where I stashed the box. As I pull it out, the note drops to the floor. I pick it up and put it on the counter to add to my tin 'TREASURES' box. I remove the ribbon from the box and open it to find the most beautiful diamond ring I have ever seen. It has a small, but beautiful, round-cut diamond on a delicate, shiny gold band.

I take it from the box and hand it to Charlie to put on my finger. As I look into Charlie's eyes, I whisper, "Yes."

Charlie smiles the biggest smile and places the ring on my finger. It's a perfect fit. Then, for the first time since I met him, he takes me in his arms and kisses me. I didn't expect his kiss to be so wonderful, but it is the most wonderful thing I have ever imagined. I have butterflies like I have never had before. "I love you, Emma."

"I love you too, Charlie."

Oh, I forgot to mention, his little note said, *Emma, now that everything worked out with the girls, please marry me. I love you, Charlie.*

"I've got to stop crying," I say.

"I don't mind."

"I do. I have to let you go because I *have* to order pizza and get some lemonade drinks before Evette and Jan get here."

"You're kicking me out?" Charlie asks with a slight hurt look on his face.

"I hate to do so, but you know I have these plans. I have to get all these gifts wrapped," I say in a *please-understand* voice. "I'd ask you to stay, but the girls will want to talk girl-talk and everything…… *and* admire my beautiful ring." I spread my left hand in front of me and show him too.

"I get it. I'll see you tomorrow?"

"Yes. In fact, can you help me get all this stuff to the orphanage? You can take the clothes now, but I need to make sure I label what belongs to whom.."

"I think I know my children," Charlie says.

"I'm sure you do. I just want to make sure.."

"I can take them now, and we can sort them out tomorrow since you're not wrapping them. By the way, are we still going to the Christmas Eve service?"

"That's the plan. We should have put the clothes in your car from my car, but no biggie. Let's do it now."

We load all the clothes and shoes and boots and hats in Charlie's car, he kisses me again, and we say goodbye.

I can't believe I have a fiancé. Who'da thought?

I return to my living room and really don't know where to begin.

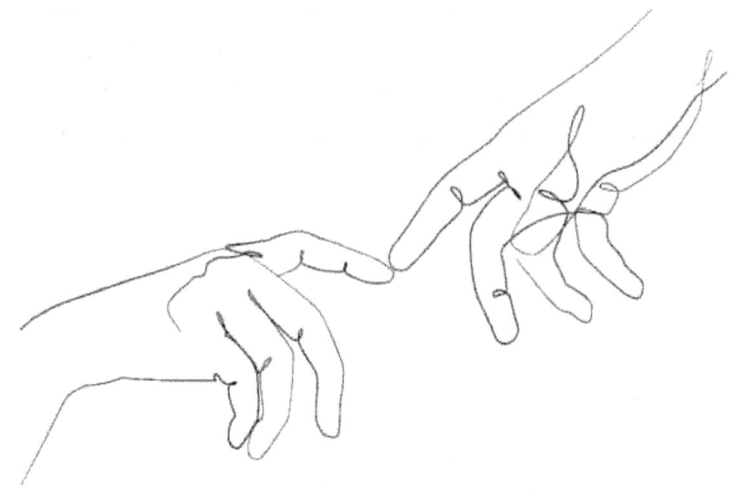

19

The Wrapping Party

Who would have thought wrapping presents would be such an ordeal? I bought ten rolls of wrapping paper to make certain we don't run out. I lined up tape and name tags in rows on my living room table. I separated the toys into seventeen piles and put a small sticker on one of the toys to remind myself whose they are. I'm exhausted, and the girls haven't even arrived.

I'm going to order a vegetable supreme pizza and pick up some lemonade and sodas. I also have peppermint cocoa and tea.

It's getting late, so I change into my comfy clothes and tie my hair up. I take out the red lipstick Ms. Westover gave me and try some on. It is bright alright, but I like it.

I jump in my car and head out to pick up the pizza and drinks. When I return home, the girls are just pulling up.

"Hey, guys. I'm so glad you could come."

"We're happy to help," Jan says.

"Anything for pizza," Evette says.

"I got some sugar-free soda for you, Jan."

"Thanks, Em. You're the best."

The girls help me carry everything inside and we set it all on the kitchen counter. "I know we're hungry, but first, let me show you what we're in for."

I take them to the living room. "WOW!" they both say at the same time.

"How did you get all this again?" Jan asks.

"The toy store donated everything on the children's wish lists for Santa," I say triumphantly.

"Good job, Em," Evette says. "This is really wonderful for those children."

"I know. This isn't all of it. The clothing store donated hats and boots and gloves and an outfit for each child. They can wear their new clothes to the Christmas Eve service."

"Where are the clothes?" Jan asks, looking around the room.

"Charlie took them to the orphanage already," I say.

"Charlie, eh?" Evette says.

"He was here when I got home with everything and, since I have to take the toys over tomorrow, he did me a favor and took the clothes today."

"Makes sense," Jan says as she and Evette make faces at each other and nod.

"You two. I also need to tell you I found a letter in the mailbox today at the cemetery…"

"But you already know it's him," Evette interrupts.

"Yes. I do. There was a small blue box too…"

"OMG!! You have a ring on!" Evette practically screams.

She and Jan grab my hand to see my beautiful ring.

"I said *YES!* And then he kissed me!"

"Aw, he kissed you?" Jan says quizzically.

"Well, yes. He's my fiancé now. It's only right that he should kiss me, isn't it?"

"Yes. But just the other day you said, '*No.*' And you two have never been on a real date, have you?"

"No. Not technically. We have carved pumpkins, planted flowers, been on a sled ride, and shared hot cocoa," I say as if we've dated for years. Mostly trying to make light of this situation.

"You're funny," Jan says.

"I know. It's more than I can process sometimes. Just a short while ago, I thought my whole world was upside-down. Now, it's all working out. I can't believe I'm going to be a mom and I have a fiancé. My life is better than I ever thought it could be."

"Did you tell Grandpapa?" Evette asks in a somewhat

mischievous tone.

"You bet I did!" I ignore her making fun of me for running to my Grandpapa for everything. "So, how about we eat some pizza and enjoy some lemonade?"

We make our way to the kitchen, and each of us grabs a plate and a napkin and digs in. It's hard to believe three girls can eat almost a whole large pizza! It reminds me of my date with Peter.

"Now I think I'm too stuffed to wrap presents," I say, rubbing my tummy.

"Me too. Let's talk for a few more minutes before we get started," Evette says.

"And you wrote a book and won an award, too? Girl, what can't you do?" Jan says.

"I can't enter a gift-wrapping contest to see who's the fastest gift wrapper after eating almost three pieces of pizza!" I exclaim. "Thanks for everything, you guys. I appreciate all the nice things you said to the adoption agency. It made a huge difference. Want to see the girls' room?"

"Sure," they say together.

We manage to get out of our chairs and walk to the girls' bedroom. Evette and Jan appreciate things as much as I do. We're kindred spirits for sure.

"How's your boyfriend, Jan?" I ask.

"Things are good. But, we're not quite as far along as you and Charlie," she replies.

"You will be," I say.

"I hope so. Happy looks so good on you, Em," Jan says.

We mosey on back to the living room. "I have plenty of wrapping paper and tape. The hard part is going to be keeping each child's gifts together. I sorted them and put the toys that belong to each child in small separate piles," I say, holding wrapping paper in one hand and tape in the other.

"We'll get it," Evette says with confidence.

I show the girls the seventeen wish lists, and we begin sorting through the toys.

"These are really nice dolls," Jan says.

"And this little baking oven is to die for!" Evette says excitedly.

"The toy store was very generous. They included everything, and it looks like a few extra things."

We spend the rest of the evening wrapping and taping and placing name stickers on each package until all the gifts are wrapped and tagged.

"I wish I was an orphan…" Jan starts to say. "Oops, I didn't mean that the way it sounded. This mechanical boat you picked for Tommy is super cool," she says quickly to pretend no one noticed her orphan comment.

"I know what you mean. I wish they could all have homes. It must be difficult. They have their rooms and are taken care of, but don't have their own televisions or someone to read to them before bed…" I trail off for a moment and then continue, "I had Grandpapa and he was and always will be the BEST!" I say, trying to make Jan's comment alright.

We finally wrap the last gift. "I can't believe it's only nine thirty," I say.

"We rocked it!" Evette says.

"What else can we help with?" Jan asks.

"You guys are really the best," I say. "Charlie's coming over tomorrow to help me take the presents to the orphanage after the children are asleep. We want them to think Ho Ho brought these gifts. They have other gifts that were donated that are under the tree already."

"Of course, these are from Santa. He got a little help from his elves, Emma, Evette, and Jan!" Jan exclaims.

"For sure," I add. "We could sit in the living room by the tree, but you can see there's no space left right now…"

"Well, we like your kitchen too," Jan says sweetly.

"The kitchen it is!" I enthuse. "I have something for each of you."

"Em, you didn't.." Jan says.

"Oh, but I did. I wanted to get something for my besties."

Jan and Evette head to the kitchen, and I retrieve an armful of boxes and set them in front of Evette.

"For me?" Evette asks.

"Yes. I'll get Jan's."

"This is too much," Jan protests.

"Nonsense," I reply.

I come back from the bedroom with another armful of boxes and set them in front of Jan. "Merry Christmas, you two."

"Em, this is too sweet of you."

The girls open their boxes and love their powder-blue cashmere sweaters, books to journal, an assortment of hand lotions, hat, scarf, and glove sets, small bottles of perfume – or pre-fume as my twins call it – and a pair of their birthstone post earrings.

"Em, these are beautiful," they both say as they 'ooh and aah' over their gifts. "These cost too much…"

"Not really. Everything was on sale. Not that you're not worth regular prices, but who can resist a sale?"

"Not you, that we know," Evette says, looking my way.

"You both mean so much to me. I appreciate all the help tonight and riding days and dance days…"

"We enjoy you too, Em," Jan says. She comes in for a hug. Evette follows.

"We don't usually exchange…"

"There's nothing I need right now," I interrupt, "and you did give me a present. You gave me my twin girls."

"When will they get to come home?" Evette asks.

"Sometime after the New Year. I wish it was Christmas morning. Wouldn't that be the best?"

"Sure. But anytime is great," Evette says.

"You'll take them anytime you can get them," Jan adds.

"That's for sure. As soon as I tell them, they'll want to come right away, so I'd better wait until I get an official date."

"When are you getting married?" Jan just had to ask.

"We didn't talk about that." I give her another hug and say, "You guys have a great Christmas. We'll make plans after the New Year."

They agree and leave. I sit in my living room, admiring all the pretty packages. Wrapping the 'pony on a stick' was a bit challenging, but that's okay; it's mostly covered.

I slip into my pajamas and call Charlie. "Hi, Charlie. Is it too late to call?"

"Never, Emma. Are you alright?" He sounds concerned.

"I'm fine. I just wanted to hear your voice before I hit the sack. We finished wrapping and tagging everything. I think you'll be impressed."

"I know I will be. I'm glad you called. What are you doing tomorrow....."

"Coming for Christmas Eve, silly," I interrupt.

"No. I mean before we have dinner?"

"I don't have any plans. Maybe the cemetery."

"Would you like to go somewhere with me?"

"*Somewhere?*" I'm suspicious.

"It's a secret. Do you trust me?"

"Yes. I'll go *somewhere* with you, Charlie Parker."

"Very funny, Emma Arnold. By the way, are you going to be Emma Parker or are you one of those women who want to be Emma Arnold-Parker or will you stay Emma Arnold?"

"You know, I really haven't given that any thought. But I like the sound of Emma Parker." I can't see him, but I think he's smiling. "I'll see you tomorrow and we'll go *somewhere,* Charlie Parker."

"Okay, Emma Arnold. See you tomorrow."

We hang up. I'm not tired, so I sit and mull over the day and everything that's going on, along with my *Gertie* book and beautiful engagement ring.

20

Somewhere With Charlie

I'm excited and nervous at the same time. Where is it Charlie wants to take me? Technically, this is our first date.

I look out my kitchen window to see two feet of newly fallen snow. I think *it sure is pretty* as the flakes continue to drift lightly and gently onto the branches of the pine trees. The squirrels have left their little footprints in paths to my feeders.

Charlie wants to surprise me for our 'first date,' and he won't tell me where we're going. Considering the weather, I wear my comfy jeans, my lamb's wool-lined boots, a white turtleneck with snowmen printed on it, and a red bulky sweater. I wear my trusty pink headband. It keeps my forehead and ears warm.

I don't wear much make-up right now because Charlie knows me well, and he doesn't seem to mind when I don't wear it. Plus, I'll wear make-up tonight for the Christmas Eve church service with the children.

Just as I tug my left boot on, I hear a knock at the door. "Coming!" I shout.

Charlie's dressed as casually as I am, and the car's still running in the drive as he comes to collect me. "Ready?" he asks.

"Yes, I am. Where're we going, Charlie?" I try asking nonchalantly.

"You'll see," Charlie says with a crooked smile.

He's driving me crazy with this mysterious *somewhere* place he's taking me, but I want to be with him.

The roads are slippery, so Charlie drives slowly. After

driving for about forty-five minutes, we finally pull into a long driveway that leads to a century home right smack dab in the middle of a three-acre front yard. The two-story house may be more than a hundred years old, but the white paint looks fresh and the grass-green shutters hang flush against the windows. A fresh cedar Christmas wreath with red bows and pine cones in it hangs on the dark oak front door.

The lamp post near the house is wrapped with pine roping and evenly spaced red ribbon bows. Snow has covered the tops of all the fence boards around the acres of pastures surrounding the house.

"What a stunningly beautiful home. Whose is it?" I ask slowly.

"This," Charlie pauses for effect just to see me squirm. "This is my grandparents' farm. They left it to me."

"*You* own *this*?"

"*Yes*. I own this."

"Why didn't you ever mention…"

"The subject never came up, and I spend most of my time at the orphanage. They have a room for me there. I almost mentioned it when you asked if the twins could ride horses with you. I have horses here and more surprises."

"I'm not sure I can take more surprises. The farm is quite a big surprise itself. And the house is beautiful."

"Yes, it is. But wait 'til you see the barn," he beams.

After we park the car, Charlie grabs a picnic basket from the back seat, then walks around to open my door.

"Thank you. What's in the basket?" I ask.

"You are just full of questions, aren't you, Miss Emma? Well, let me spare you any more anxiety. I packed a picnic lunch and we're going to take a sleigh ride through the woods on the other side of the large pasture, and…"

"What a perfect idea for our first real date."

"I thought long and hard about what to plan for us. I wanted it to be special. How'm I doing?"

"Great. It's romantic." I smile. "Just like you."

We make our way through the soft, fluffy, freshly fallen

snow to the barn. It's an eight-stall structure with rod iron tops over the board-bottom stalls. Cast iron sconces line the walls of the barn and the floor is patterned concrete.

Charlie sets the picnic basket on a chair in the aisleway of the barn and opens one of the stalls. He calls out, "Bubba," and a large dark brown gelding comes to him. Charlie places a halter over his head and attaches a lead line.

Bubba walks out of his stall like a gentleman and Charlie puts him in cross-ties. These are lines attached to the walls that connect to the horse on both sides of his halter to keep him standing in the aisle.

Charlie places a harness over Bubba's back and replaces his halter with a bridle with long lines that run through rings on the harness so he can drive the horse in the sleigh.

I follow Charlie outside, where he pulls a white antique sleigh from the overhang next to the barn. It looks like a sleigh from a fairy tale with gold trim and a red velvet seat. He sets it in the freshly fallen snow, and then we walk Bubba to the sleigh. I hold him as Charlie attaches the sleigh to the harness with straps on both sides of the harness.

"Wow," I say.

"Do you like it?"

"Oh, yes."

"Let's get in and go for a ride."

Charlie helps me onto the seat and climbs in next to me. Although the snow is still falling lightly, there's very little wind. The cold still has a little bite to it, but it isn't unbearable. Charlie's prepared with a heavy woolen blanket he spreads over our legs.

Charlie drives the sleigh like he was born in one. He holds each line in his hands, softly taps Bubba's rump, and clucks to him. Bubba begins walking. We head down the lane past the pastures and the bells to the harness jingle as we trot along.

"I wanted you to see this farm so you know I can take care of you."

"I know you can. I never doubted that. It's beautiful here," I'm not exactly sure what Charlie wants me to know.

"We can live in your house, or here."

"I never considered moving from my home, but we can certainly talk about all this. I admit I have always wanted to live on a farm," I say as I look at him sincerely. I'm torn about this. It'll take a little time for me to decide what to do.

We continue our ride down trails between towering pine trees, all blanketed with snow. Charlie knows the snow-covered paths we take, and we ride in silence for a few minutes. As we pass some of the pines, we hit the longer branches and snow flies onto us, "Oh, my," I say as I wipe the snow away.

"This time of year is short, but one I enjoy very much. It's not *as* cold *as* it will be in a month or so, and the snow is clean and soft. I have so many memories of riding this sleigh in the new snow," Charlie says, breaking the silence.

"What wonderful memories. The girls will love this."

"I think so too. I wanted our first date to be memorable."

"I'll never forget today. I'm so happy, Charlie. Thank you for everything."

"Thank you for saying '*Yes.*' I'm happy too."

I take his arm in mine and ask, "When did you learn to drive the sleigh?"

"*My* grandpapa taught me when I was a young boy. Sleigh rides were always a special part of our Christmas and winter traditions."

"How wonderful. I'm glad we both have fond memories of Grandpapas." I snuggle a little as we head back to the barn. "What's for lunch?" I ask. I didn't have much for breakfast since I didn't know what to expect.

"I'll show you. Let's get Bubba untacked and back in his stall."

We take the sleigh off the horse's harness and then remove the harness. We trade the bridle for his halter and return him to his stall. While Charlie wipes Bubba's hair down, I help myself to a flake of hay for him. I thank Bubba for the ride as I pat his neck. He dips his head to enjoy his newly delivered treat.

"Let's go over here," Charlie says as he begins walking to a small picnic table with a layer of snow on top of it.

He sweeps the snow off the table and benches with his

gloved hands. We sit for our *gourmet* meal.

"Here's for you," Charlie says, handing me a sandwich.

"What's this?..." I ask as I open the wrapping - a peanut butter and jelly sandwich. I smile. "This is perfect." Peanut butter and jelly just happens to be my favorite take-along sandwich and I'm happy to have it.

"It's your fave, isn't it?" Charlie asks with a wink, mimicking the way I say *'fave.'*

"All kidding aside, peanut butter and jelly *is* my *fave.*" I begin eating as Charlie hands me a thermos with hot cocoa. *Another* of my faves! "Seems you thought of everything, Charlie."

"Like I said, I wanted our first date to be special," he says as he takes a bite of his peanut butter and jelly sandwich.

"I love this farm. I didn't know you knew about horses either. Maybe I don't know enough about you, Charlie," I say, slightly uncertain if we've made the right decision. Suddenly I begin to think about what is *his* favorite sandwich? What is *his* favorite color? Did he go to college? Did he ever have another girlfriend?.....

"We know enough about each other to know we're meant to be together. We have a lifetime to learn everything about each other and blend our lives together," he assures me, interrupting my runaway thoughts.

"That makes me feel better," I say, relieved. "I guess there are things about me you don't know. But since you've read all my letters to Grandpapa, I'm not sure what that could be. I haven't kept any secrets from you."

"The farm isn't really a secret. I just never mentioned it. When you went on that date with Peter, I thought I didn't have a chance. But life has a way of working out."

"I'm glad it worked out this way."

We finish our sandwiches and Charlie says, "Now for dessert."

"Cheesecake. Another of my faves," I say as he hands me a piece of tiramisu-flavored cheesecake with chocolate syrup drizzled on top on a paper plate with a plastic fork.

We pack up the basket and take a walk around the barn to visit the other horses. I have only dreamt of keeping a horse in a barn this beautiful. *This is spectacular,* I think to myself.

We drive home more slowly because the plow trucks haven't gotten to the roads yet, and the snow is still falling. If this keeps up, it'll be a good thing church is within walking distance of the orphanage.

"I'm looking forward to seeing the children in their new clothes and going to candlelight service tonight," I say.

"We had the children try on their clothes, and they all fit. I forgot to tell you how much the children like what you got them. Some of them have never had new clothes in their life – only hand-me-downs."

"I'm glad to know they like the clothes. I love them and want them to have nice things like other children."

"That's what I cherish most about you, Em. You have so much love in your heart." Charlie gives my hand a tender squeeze.

When we arrive home, Charlie offers to help load all the presents, "My car is bigger than yours, Em. So, let me take the presents with me. I can hide them, and we can put them under the tree after the children go to bed."

"I appreciate your help."

We load all the presents we can in Charlie's car. There are only a few that won't fit.

"I can bring these when I come. The cold won't bother these, and we can keep them in my car until after they go to bed." I kiss Charlie and say, "See you in a couple of hours."

"Can't wait."

21

Christmas Eve

I had the best time with Charlie and take a moment to start jotting a little letter about it all for Grandpapa. I can't believe Charlie owns a farm, and horses too!

I don't have much time since it took all morning and early afternoon to visit Charlie's farm, so I quickly put on my make-up. I don't usually wear make-up to the orphanage, but I do for special occasions. I go light on the blush and use my soft blue eye shadow. My new red lipstick Ms. Westover gave me is my new fave, so I pucker up and put that on too!

I change clothes so I'm dressed for church. I bought a new red dress and have white hose and red slipper shoes to match my new beautiful dress. I add pearl earrings with my matching pearl necklace. I spray a little Shalimar perfume over my neck and make sure my hair is tied up out of my face. I wear my black cashmere coat and red gloves and wrap my red, white, and green scarf around my neck.

After dropping in on Grandpapa and leaving my letter, I head to the orphanage. As I stand in the day room, I take a moment to soak in all the marvelous Christmas decorations. The ginormous live tree we brought back a few weeks ago is still in good shape, and the fragrance of pine fills the air.

The tree decorations are complete with ornaments the children have made over the years as well as the ornaments the orphanage had stored away. There are pinecones with pictures glued on them, hearts with their names written in glitter glue, popsicle stick snowmen, and multi-colored lights and strands of popcorn are strung meticulously over each branch. It really is looking a lot like Christmas!

Every year, the community generously donates gifts so every child has a present to open on Christmas morning. The staff placed the colorfully wrapped boxes underneath the tree with the names of the children written on attached tags. Charlie once told me how the children eagerly open their gifts on Christmas Eve and can't wait to see what Ho Ho brings on Christmas Day!

I particularly think the pine roping with red bows and silver bells wrapped around the banisters are enchanting. It's like something out of a Christmas movie. This is one of the things I love most about this orphanage - they make the holidays and every day something extraordinary for the children.

As Charlie comes into the day room, I ask, "Where did you hide the presents?"

"They're in the conference room. The children don't go in there," he says warmly.

Mrs. Carter follows Charlie into the room. "Emma, I need to see you in my office, please. Charlie, please join us."

Am I in trouble? Did I do too much this year? Is there a problem with the adoption? So many thoughts run through my mind as I follow Mrs. Carter to her office.

"Please sit," Mrs. Carter motions to me.

She shuffles papers for a few minutes, then looks up and says, "Emma. I want to tell you how happy I am about the adoption...."

"I want to thank you so much," I interrupt.

"It is my pleasure to help you and the girls. That's not all I wanted to share with you."

"Oh?"

"Yes. I want to be the one to tell you I'm retiring after the holidays. Charlie will be taking over my position. I'm sure he will continue the great work here."

I look at Charlie. He isn't surprised, so I realize he knew about this before this meeting.

"Now, there are a few more steps to finalize the adoption, of course," Mrs. Carter says matter-of-factly.

"Of course," I repeat.

"We'll have Christmas Eve and Christmas Day celebrations, and everything should be complete before the New Year."

"Ok," is all I can manage to say. "When do you think I should tell Sarah and Susan?"

"After everything is finalized, please. Well, Merry Christmas, Emma." Mrs. Carter smiles warmly.

I stand and leave, but Charlie stays a few more minutes. I'm floating as I walk to the day room. Sarah and Susan run to me and leap into the air. This can be a trick if I don't catch them, so I stoop to make sure they each land in my arms. "Hello, little girls!" I exclaim.

"Merry Kissmas," they say together.

"Merry Christmas to you, too," I say and twirl them as they giggle.

Charlie comes to my rescue and takes Susan. "Mr. Charlie!" she shouts as he twirls her. "Merry Kissmmass!"

All the children join us in the day room. The boys are wearing their ties and look like little gentlemen in their white button shirts. The girls twirl in their pretty dresses and new patent leather shoes with their ankle socks. The older girls look lovely in their dresses and tights. "You are all lovely," I say with a smile.

"Thank you for the new clothes, Emma," Annette says and gives me a hug.

"My pleasure, angel," I say.

Each child thanks me. I tell them I'm glad they like the clothes, and that we're going to have a wonderful Christmas Eve and we will see what Santa brings tomorrow morning.

"I think we'll open these presents later tonight, after the service," Charlie says, pointing to the donated presents already under the tree. "*Then* we'll see what Ho Ho brings tomorrow."

"Yeah!!" the children say together.

"We got these presents donated," Tony informs me.

"I know," I say as I take him in my arms for a hug. "You'll be so surprised when you open them."

"Let's all get to the cafeteria for dinner," Charlie says, showing the children the way. Then he looks at me and says, "I hope they look this good after their meal."

"They will," I say, more hoping than knowing.

We all sit around the table and Charlie says grace.

All the children say a loud, "AMEN!"

Thankfully, the cooks have prepared food that isn't messy. We have little chicken nuggets and tater tots. All finger foods. The children also have milk, and no one spills a drop. It's a Christmas Eve miracle for sure.

"We'll save dessert for after church when we change into our night clothes. Let's get our coats and hats on," Charlie says to the children.

"And our gloves," Tony says as he puts his gloves on.

"Yes. Thank you for reminding me, Anthony," Charlie says. He only calls him 'Anthony' sometimes.

The children line up nicely. There's a little talking about what's in the wrapped presents under the tree, but very little fidgeting about this evening.

As we walk to the church just across the street from the orphanage, I lead the children in "We Wish You a Merry Christmas."

The ushers escort us to the last two pews reserved for us. As we take our seats, the usher hands each adult and older child a wax candle and each of the younger children a battery-operated candle. Charlie directs Annette to sit on the opposite end of the pew to watch the children, and then sits next to me.

When all the rows are filled, people are given chairs to sit in the aisle next to the pews. The lights dim, and the service begins with a prayer of thanks for the Christmas Season and the birth of Baby Jesus.

The children lift their voices as we all sing *Hark the Herald Angels*. Our children sound like angels to Charlie and me. They must be enjoying the music because they're barely fidgeting tonight.

We listen as a young girl sings a solo of one of the most famous Christmas songs, *O, Holy Night*. She takes a huge breath and belts out those high notes perfectly. The whole church softly applauds her singing.

The service concludes with everyone lighting their candles and singing *Silent Night*. Charlie holds my hand, and Susan and Sarah stand on the pew next to us.

As we file out of the church, the ushers pass out small bags with treats for the children. They smile and bring their treat bags with them as we get them dressed in their coats and hats and head back to the orphanage.

The younger children are tired, and a few fall asleep before we can open presents and have our snacks. Charlie carries Joey, Annette takes Sarah, and I take Susan. The older children help get a few others to their rooms. We help them into their pajamas. The older children return with us to the day room.

The cooks have left pie and cheesecake for dessert. "Would you like a piece of pie, Emma?" Charlie asks.

"No. Thank you. I'm stuffed."

We gather on the floor around the tree, and Charlie gives the go-ahead for the children to search the tags for their names. Annette 'oohs' and 'aahs' over her designer purse. "It's Gucci!" she exclaims with a big smile.

"I see," I say. "It's very nice." I do think it is nice of someone to donate such a beautiful purse.

John opens his gift that is obviously a mountain bike. "How did someone know I wanted one of these?" he asks.

"I don't know, John. But it's a very nice bike." Charlie shoots me a wink.

The older children are great and stuff their wrapping paper into large plastic bags as they open their presents, so there's not too much to clean up. Some of the girls keep the ribbons that are too pretty to throw away. We say *goodnight* and they head to their rooms.

"It's been a big day. I'm pretty tired," I say to Charlie.

"I'll help get the gifts from your car," he reminds me.

"Oh, yeah. I almost forgot."

We take the last few gifts from my car and place them under the tree. Charlie and a few assistants bring the rest of the presents that Charlie brought over from the conference room. There are brightly colored packages under the tree, on the floor, tables, and even the chairs are piled with boxes and bags tied with shiny ribbons. It looks like my living room all over again.

I can't wait to see the looks on all those sweet little faces when they walk into the room on Christmas morning.

22

Christmas Day

As the sun comes up this Christmas morning, I stay in bed a little longer, thinking just how lucky I am. I had the world's best Grandpapa, I'm going to be a mother to two beautiful twin girls, I love being a librarian, I'm an award-winning author, a musician, a dancer, and an artist! And, best of all, I have someone who loves me and wants to share everything with me. I really couldn't ask for more. I need to write a letter to Paw.

I don't eat breakfast because I'm having breakfast with Charlie and the children. Plus, there'll be a Christmas feast to enjoy with the children and Charlie.

I wear my Christmas Eve red dress and am still wearing my pearl earrings and pearl necklace. I refresh my makeup and put on my white hose. I spray a spritz of fresh perfume over my neck and make sure my hair is tied up out of my face. I wear my same black cashmere coat and red gloves, and wrap my red, white, and green scarf around my neck.

It snowed more last night, giving everyone a very white Christmas. I wear my boots to the cemetery and will change to my slipper shoes at the orphanage. "Off to see Grandpapa," I say to myself.

I drive to see Paw and park. Charlie's here. "I wasn't expecting to see you here today."

"I debated on whether to see you here or wait until you came to the orphanage. I decided to meet you here."

"I'm here. Do you want to read my letter to my grandfather?"

"You're funny." We stand motionless for a moment, and then Charlie continues, "Well, sure."

I hand him the note and he reads it out loud as I blush.

Dear Paw, It's Christmas. It's never the same without you. I'm planning on having Christmas breakfast and lunch at the orphanage. I can't wait to bring the girls home for the first time. It will be soon. I decorated their room. They each have a beautiful, small white bed. They also each have their own dresser and little vanity. I put stuffed animals on their beds and they have night lights that make the light scatter over the walls and ceiling. I put pictures of them and the other children from the orphanage on the walls. I'm so excited. I can't tell them until it's all final. I told Charlie I will marry him…..

He lowers the note, and we hug. He's the man I've waited for all my life.

"Let me finish…..

…..I love him. He's like you in so many ways, Paw. He's patient and kind and loves children. He loves me. I can feel it and know it every time he looks at me and spends time with me. You would love him too. I also wanted you to know I believe I will be a great mom. I know I'm not the best artist or musician or dancer or writer or gardener, but I love these things and will always do my best and enjoy them, no matter if I'm better or worse than others. Thank you for loving me, Grandpapa, and thank you for always being here for me.
Merry Christmas, Love, Emma.

"This is quite beautiful, Emma."

"And what note would you write me back and put in my little mailbox?" I ask with an expectant expression.

"Well. I would say again and again, "Thank you for saying, '*Yes*.' I do love you and promise to make you happy forever. I want you to know that when I take Mrs. Carter's position, I'll not only have you and Sarah and Susan, I'll be Papa to all the children there and I hope you will be Mama to them too." He smiles that smile I love so much.

"Well, I always wanted to take them all home."

"We have lots of time to work out all the details. Sarah and Susan will be home with you soon. Hopefully, we'll marry soon. Then we can decide everything else. Let's go to Christmas with our kids."

"Ok."

Charlie puts his arm around me, and it feels like the most natural thing in the world.

We arrive at the orphanage to happy children. "Can we open our presents?" Tina asks.

"Yeah, can we?" the others ask.

"Yes! You may open your presents," Charlie says.

We decide to let them find their piles and open them all at once. It's bedlam, but they do a good job throwing the paper in a large trash can we placed in the room.

They show us their presents and are so happy to have received the gifts on their lists. "I even got my fire truck," Tony says with a big smile.

"I see," I say and give him a hug.

"I like these *pre-fumes*," Susan says, showing them to me.

"Me too," Sarah agrees and shows me hers as well.

"Who's hungry?" I ask.

They all say, "ME!" at once.

We make pancakes today. Charlie and I take over the cooks' kitchen. I mix as he pours and fries the small pancakes we make quickly on all the stove burners so as many children as possible can have their pancakes at the same time. The older children help with breakfast. They pour the syrup so we don't have sticky over all the tables and chairs and younger children.

The children spend hours playing with their new toys, and we have small Christmas cookies and red and green popcorn balls for them to snack on in the day room.

After hours of play, we gather for Christmas dinner. The cooks prepared turkey and ham before they left yesterday to enjoy their families. They added macaroni and cheese for the children who don't care for turkey or ham. They're so thoughtful. "Let's save the pie for later, ok?" I suggest this because we have eaten more than usual.

"Yeah!" the children shout in agreement.

After our meal settles, the children put their coats and hats and boots and gloves on and ask to go outside. It's still light, so Charlie, the older children, and I also put my warm clothes on to join them. I'm glad I brought a change of clothes.

The children play in the drifts and try to make snowballs to throw gently at each other. But the snow is too soft. They laugh as they try to throw snowballs at Charlie. "Bring it!" he exclaims and tries to make snowballs to throw at each of them. The snow merely falls apart before it can reach its target.

We all lay in the snow and made snow angels like we did when we went sledding. The little angels are adorable when Susan and Sarah stand to show me theirs.

Brian hides from the others, so they have to find him. Hide and seek ensues. Charlie joins in and hides behind one of the trees in the yard. Tony finds him. Sarah and Susan don't let me out of their sight, so it's impossible for me to hide. I try taking them to hide with me, but Joey finds us right away because the girls chatter endlessly, giving away our hiding spot.

Sarah and Susan talk me into making snowmen. They are short, so the snowmen are small and have only two parts to their bodies and head instead of the normal three parts.

When the children run out of steam, we all come back inside. We sit around the table and have dessert. Each child chooses apple or cherry pie and pumpkin pie. We remember how we like our whipped cream sprayed right into our mouths as well as on our pie!

After dessert, I find Sarah and Susan in their room. "Girls, can we talk?" I say.

This is the best Christmas ever. I need to give Charlie his gift as well.

Mother Gertie : A Mother Goose is a picture book created by author, Terrie Sizemore. It is based on her own goose who did not have goslings but did mother five ducklings the two duck mothers hatched.

It is a 5-Star award winning Reader's Choice book and is available on Amazon.

About the Author

Terrie Sizemore has been publishing and writing since 2008. She enjoys children's literature, particularly children's picture books.

She decided to write this little book about letters to Grandpapa because she identifies with so much of the story.

Over the years, the author has lost her parents, her brothers, uncles, aunts, and treasured friends. Even though her faith tells her she will see these loved ones again, she misses each and every one of them and knows every reader misses their loved ones as well.

"We read to know we're not alone," was a quote Terrie Sizemore heard in a C. S. Lewis movie. She agrees. It's nice to know we're not alone in our journey of life.

Sometimes it's nice to feel connected to the ones we have lost. Terrie wishes she did have a mailbox by the site where her beloved Grandpapa's body is resting. She knows he knows what's in her heart and still watches out for her every day. She owes him everything and never wants to forget how much he means to her.